PENGUIN BOOKS
BHAVA

U.R. Anantha Murthy, one of the most influential representatives of the 'navya' (modernist) movement in Kannada literature, was born in Melige village, Karnataka, in 1932. He was trained in a traditional Sanskrit school, and earned his BA and MA in English at Mysore University.

In 1963, he went to England on a Commonwealth Fellowship. While pursuing Ph.D. studies at the University of Birmingham, he wrote his controversial first novel, *Samskara*. Published in 1965, it was a sensation in the world of Kannada letters. *Samskara* has been translated into many languages, and made into an award-winning film. Anantha Murthy's other publications include two novels, *Bharathipura* and *Avasthe*, and volumes of short stories, poems, and essays. Two of his stories, 'Bara' and 'Ghatashraddha,' have appeared in film versions.

Anantha Murthy has been Professor of English at Mysore University, and he has taught and lectured widely outside India. He has served as Vice-Chancellor of Mahatma Gandhi University, Kerala; Chairman of the National Book Trust of India, and President of the Sahitya Akademi. His many honours and awards include the Masti Award in Literature, the Jnanpith Award, and Padma Bhushan.

*

Judith Kroll, American poet, essayist, and translator, lived in India for many years. Author of two collections of poetry, a book of literary criticism, and numerous contributions to magazines and journals, she teaches poetry writing at the University of Texas at Austin, where she is also affiliated with the Center for Asian Studies.

U.R. Anantha Murthy

BHAVA

Translated from the Kannada by
Judith Kroll with the author

PENGUIN BOOKS

Penguin Books India (P) Ltd., 210 Chiranjiv Tower, 43 Nehru Place, New Delhi 110 019 India
Penguin Books Ltd., 27 Wrights Lane, London W8 5TZ, UK
Penguin Books USA Inc., 375 Hudson Street, New York, New York 10014, USA
Penguin Books Australia Ltd., Ringwood, Victoria, Australia
Penguin Books Canada Ltd., 10 Alcorn Avenue, Suite 300, Toronto, Ontario, MAV 3B2, Canada
Penguin Books (NZ) Ltd., 182-190 Wairau Road, Auckland, 10, New Zealand

First published in Kannada by Akshara Prakashna, Sagara, Karnataka 1994
Copyright © U.R. Anantha Murthy 1994

First published in English by Penguin Books India (P) Ltd. 1998
This translation copyright © Judith Kroll 1998

Typeset in *PalmSprings* by SÜRYA, New Delhi-110 011

Contents

Contents

Author's Note

Bhava, like many of my other narratives, is a tale, although in its overall intention it is unlike any previous work of mine. Translating a tale in which an author aspires to the organic coherence and denseness of a poem in the language of its genesis makes one nervous and uncertain, for it doesn't possess the easily shared exterior of conventional realistic fiction. I feel fortunate that a poet translated the work with me, for I found her sensitive to the intended nuances in the original text.

We went about our work in this fashion. I would do a literal translation of the original into English, often word for word, keeping intact even the sentence structures peculiar to my Kannada. Then I would talk about the form and meaning and subtleties of the passage. Judith Kroll would record my free renderings and then prepare from her notes and tapes an English version for my perusal.

As a teacher of English, for many years I used English for discursive purposes. But my creative efforts were always in Kannada. This switching between two languages constantly had been a stressful experience. It was only when I collaborated on this translation that to some extent I ventured to use English for creative purposes. In the process, I learnt a great deal about what it is for the author of an original work in one language to collaborate with another writer and to see that work reborn in another language.

The process of translating *Bhava* was also a chastening experience. I had taken for granted that my Kannada had adequately mediated what I wanted to convey. When I worked to convey the same experience in another language I became aware of the imprecisions, adjectival excesses, and so on, in the original. Therefore, while trying to put my original work into English, I have made some changes in it.

The writing of *Bhava* was a new experience, for I found myself probing into regions hitherto unexplored by me. I had to do this tentatively, giving up a privileged point of view.

I hope what I did in the Kannada will be conveyed to my English readers as well, through the efforts of a writer in English who showed remarkable patience and attention to detail in this undertaking.

New Delhi
1997

Translator's Note

'Bhava,' derived from the Sanskrit root bhu, 'to be,' means both 'being' and 'becoming,' each containing the seed of the other. These two interwoven meanings frame Anantha Murthy's tale. Additional meanings—'turning into,' 'life,' 'worldly existence,' 'the world,' 'continuity of becoming (with Buddhists)' (i.e., rebirth)—also inform the story.

The Afterword could as well be read as an Introduction, particularly by those who do not mind, or may enjoy, a substantial preview of the plot (in this case, it involves what appears to be a murder). I have made a number of comparisons with Anantha Murthy's best-known work, *Samskara*, because of intriguing thematic overlapping, and because it offers an excellent example of the social consciousness and iconoclasm which has marked his earlier novels, from which *Bhava* is a departure. The Afterword may also be of interest in suggesting resonances of the new direction taken by *Bhava*.

A note about notes. My intention was to make *Bhava* accessible without weighting it like a textbook. So the 'Selected Glossary' is fairly selective. I have not given definitions for a number of words ('guru,' 'mantra,' 'darshan') that may be familiar to many non-Indian readers, or whose general sense can readily be inferred; or for some words (such as those designating foods, holidays, festivals, deities) whose category is clear, and which in their particulars have only an incidental bearing on the story. A gloss is provided when knowing more about a word ('kuttavalakki,' 'Shri Chakra') amplifies an area of meaning in the story; or when omitting a gloss (as for 'Emden Boat') might leave a puzzling gap. In saying all this, I reveal a preference for leaving certain words in the Indian languages, at least some of the time, rather than translating every occurrence into English— particularly when a limited translation might impart a noticeable cultural charge or connotation ('rosary' for mala; 'renunciation' for vairagya).

Several remarks Anantha Murthy made in the course of translating this work have been interpolated into the Afterword. ('Anantha Murthy has commented . . .,' for example, indicates such usage.)

My own knowledge of Kannada is slight, though three years of formal Sanskrit study have been a considerable help, since many of the significant words in *Bhava* are Sanskrit. But this translation could not, obviously, have been done by me alone. That my collaborator was the author is my punya.

In part, I took courage and encouragement from the collaboration between Edward C. Dimock, Jr. and the poet Denise Levertov (*In Praise of Krishna: Songs from the Bengali*), and that between Shri Purohit Swami and W.B. Yeats (*Ten Principal Upanishads*).

I am grateful to several of my friends in Shimla: I had useful discussions with Prof. T.N. Dhar, who also read a draft of the Afterword and made small suggestions that yielded big results; my neighbours Shyama Sharma and Anita Chauhan gave me food and affectionate friendship.

M.S. Sathyu, who has encouraged me in all my Kannada-English translation projects, read an early draft of *Bhava* and made helpful remarks.

The India International Centre in New Delhi provided a hospitable atmosphere in which some of this work was done.

Grateful thanks are due to the Center for Asian Studies at The University of Texas at Austin for funds that enabled Anantha Murthy to come to Austin and work for a time on this project; additional funding was provided by the university's Texas Center for Writers.

Shimla
July 1997

BOOK ONE

BOOK ONE

1

Bhava: . . . becoming, turning into . . . being, state of being . . . worldly existence . . .
—*A Sanskrit-English Dictionary,*
Sir M. Monier-Williams

When Vishwanatha Shastri's eyes fell on the amulet around the neck of the man sitting opposite, he felt as if a demon had entered him. Had a sign suddenly been revealed to him? The man wearing the amulet was sitting, legs folded, in an easy posture, delicately picking sprouts from a steel box. One by one, he would place the sprouts between his slightly open lips and move his chin as if he were eating ambrosia. Shastri also observed two other men sitting on the torn cushions of the first-class compartment. But the man wearing the amulet sat as if unaware of anyone else, his eyes looking out on thorny bushes, crows crying thirstily, and buffaloes dozing in the scant shade of their own making.

Clearly the man opposite Shastri had taken the vow of Ayyappa—he was wearing a black kurta, a black dhoti, a small black towel over his shoulder; and against these black clothes the amulet around his neck compelled attention.

Shastri occupied the window seat. He had a scraggly white beard, since he shaved only once a month, and he wore a green-bordered white cloth shawl wrapped around his upper body, as well as a dhoti with a matching border. He looked to be about seventy. The other two men wore pants and shirts. Only Shastri and the Ayyappa pilgrim, because of their traditional dress, appeared remarkable in the first-class compartment.

It was afternoon. The two men dressed in pants and shirts had got their food from the station. One man in jeans, a meat-eater, did not want to discomfort either the Ayyappa devotee in his black clothes, or Shastri (who wore tulsi leaves in his top-knot), so he had climbed to the upper berth and, bent double, stealthily sucked at the bones. The other man who wore pants—but had kumkum on his forehead—was mixing rice with sambar, kneading it into a ball, popping it into his mouth, and chewing noisily.

Shastri brought out a steel box from the deerskin-covered bundle in which he kept his ritually pure things. He began sweating and trembling so badly that he could not open the cover of the box. His eyes kept staring at the amulet, trying to comprehend the sign that teased him like a riddle.

Was the wearer of the amulet middle-aged, or younger than that? There were one or two white hairs in his black beard. He looked fit for the role of Rama or Krishna in a play, such were the qualities of his face. Drained, yet full of lustre. His well-shaped nostrils, the colour of his large eyes, the attractiveness of his indifferent gaze—these were so like Saroja's that Shastri, recognizing this, was thunderstruck. A deep tenderness welled up in him, and even many days later he would call this moment to mind as a way of warding off evil omens.

As the Ayyappa pilgrim sat chewing sprouted lentils, he looked to Shastri like a tender calf passively receiving sunshine and rain on its body. And now his cup must be empty . . . his eyes looked down expectantly. Shastri could not bear it. He was surprised at the compassion which rose up in him. So, opening his own round steel box, he braced himself on his left arm, shifted on the seat, brought the box closer to the younger man, and held it out. Not comfortable addressing him with the intimacy of the singular, he said, using the plural, 'Please take some.'

From the questioning way that the man looked at Shastri, it was clear that he did not know Kannada. Shastri felt relieved: the man must be someone other than who he imagined. All at once, it occurred to Shastri that he could use his Hindustani, learned in Bombay some forty or forty-five years ago in his days of wayward living. But he hesitated to speak in such a rough language to an Ayyappa devotee.

Then came another surprise. The devotee began to move his fingers in his beard and seemed suddenly unsettled. As if slowly recognizing what was held out to him he said, in a wavering voice, kut-ta-va-lak-ki.

Shastri felt his hair stand on end when he heard this word, which came to him as if from an ancient cave. In the manner of someone beginning a conversation with an assumed familiarity, Shastri said, 'Then you know what this is. If you know this as kut-ta-va-lak-ki then you must be from South Kanara, or at some time must have got mixed up with somebody like me. When I do harikatha, I sometimes say: "Kuchela must be from South Kanara, because although he was a poor classmate of Krishna's, he brought Krishna not just avalakki but kuttavalakki." ' Although Shastri felt confident using the language to which he was accustomed, he also felt uneasy because his words did not connect to what he was feeling inside. But the young man folded his hands respectfully, like one who did not understand anything, and his self-absorbed eyes communicated to Shastri, 'Leave me alone.' But just as those distant eyes began once again to discomfort Shastri, the young man said 'achcha' and held out his hand for the kuttavalakki. Shastri poured it affectionately into the palm of his hand, and the young man put it in his mouth. As he chewed the kuttavalakki with closed eyes, he seemed to be trying to recover some distant memory . . . and this created in Shastri both hope and fear.

*

By this time, the man in jeans had finished his meal and said in English, 'May I know your name?' to the Ayyappa devotee. But the devotee did not respond. Only for Shastri did he open his eyes and Shastri, seeing tears in them, asked anxiously in Kannada, 'Was it too hot?' Then he repeated the question in Hindustani. For the first time the young man smiled and shook his head.

The meat-eater went out of the cabin, and came back drying his hands on a handkerchief which he took from the pocket of his jeans. Then he repeated his question more politely, 'May I please know your name?'

But the Ayyappa devotee wiped his eyes, pointed at his black clothes, and said 'Swami,' adding flatly, 'I have lost any other name.'

But the man didn't give up. 'Do you think I cannot recognize you in that dress? You are Dinakar, you are famous because of your TV shows—for my brother you are a big hero. Everyone has seen your interviews of Asian leaders. I was staring at you all along in disbelief because you didn't seem to be the sort to go after gods. But then, it seems that even Amitabh Bachchan has had darshan of Ayyappa. As soon as you got on the train in Madras, I began to wonder because you looked familiar. You must have been visiting the temples around Madras. You must be from Delhi. It is at least a whole month since I saw you on TV. I kept quiet so long because I thought it was impolite to stare at you. I am from Bombay. I deal in designer clothes. I had come to Madras to buy stock.' With this, the man wearing jeans held out his hand and, pleased with himself for having recognized Dinakar, lost none of his enthusiasm when the Ayyappa devotee failed to reciprocate. He simply continued his chat with the smooth-shaven, smiling hero who wore lovely shirts on TV.

'My daughter is doing MBBS. I must get your autograph for her. You are getting down in Bangalore, aren't you? I will take your autograph later on.'

Confident that he would eventually get the autograph, the jeans-clad man opened an English magazine and sat in the seat opposite.

Shastri kept looking at the Ayyappa devotee without blinking his eyelids, holding out the steel box as if waiting for some further signs. Now he understood that this devotee who preferred to be called only 'Swami' was a famous man from TV. He was pleased that the man was looking with interest at his kuttavalakki. Shastri opened up another container, one full of curds, and said, 'Wash your feet and hands and eat this.'. Although Swami didn't understand Shastri's language, he understood the intention. He went out of the cabin. Shastri then took out his rudraksha beads and began to do japa, feeling solace that what had entered him was not an evil spirit.

*

The other man sitting in the compartment, having finished his meal and now applying lime to his paan, began to seek conversation with Shastri. 'I know that you are the famous kirtanakar Vishwanatha Shastri. I am also from your area. My grandfather, in his time, lost his areca-nut garden and left home. You might have heard the story of the Emden Boat. Because of this we had to give up agriculture and take to business. My business in Malnad is buying and selling areca. If you are a Shivalli Smrta, I am a Shivalli Madhva. I have heard your harikatha. The way you sing and describe Sri Krishna Paramatma, we can just see him. It is my punya that I saw you.' So saying, he offered the bag with the paan utensils to Shastri. Opening his eyes, still holding his rudraksha beads, Shastri said, 'I have not yet finished my night meal.'

'But you are giving away your food to him— what will remain for you? Shall I bring some idlis for you when we reach the next station?'

'I don't take food from hotels. When I travel I carry some curds and avalakki. Even after sharing with him, I will have some left over. Anyhow, I'm grateful to you for your offer. May I know your good name?' Shastri said, happy to return to his own language.

2

Later, in moments of need, Shastri would get strength from remembering how—in pain he couldn't fully understand—he had watched Swami eating, with great appetite, the plateful of curd and beaten rice. Some door which had been closed was suddenly open. He began to feel afraid. While Shastri was searching for bananas in his deerskin bundle, the Ayyappa devotee, who was looking more and more like a true swami to him, searched in his own bag for bananas and apples and grapes. He took them out with his left hand, placed them on the seat, and with his right hand gestured to say, 'Take these.' 'Must be from a good traditional family,' Shastri thought. Shastri couldn't be certain whether his reply to Swami in the rude Bombay Hindi of his previous life was appropriate for the feelings that Swami's Hindi expressed. 'Are you full, Swami?' he asked.

There was a pause. Then Swami said softly, 'You must call me Dinakar, you are my elder.' Shastri, hearing these soft hesitant words, felt as if he were receiving punya from a previous birth, and it swept away his fear of hell.

'From your kuttavalakki I remembered the name Mother used to call me, "Putani," ' Dinakar said. 'What does Putani mean? If the name suits me, call me by that name.'

When the man dressed in fashionable jeans heard this conversation, he closed his *India Today*, laughed and said, this time in Hindi, 'Achcha, my guess was right, then.' Then he returned to his magazine.

Dinakar, to enable Shastri to understand, began to speak in Hindi slowly and simply.

'I have heard that my mother was from Kannada country. When I was five, she died in the Ganga at Hardwar. Many years later, because of a friend's mother, I remembered that my own mother fed me kuttavalakki, for I loved it very much. And now your kindness has brought that back to me. As for my father, I don't know who he was. I might have lost him earlier than I lost my mother.

Now, I have been trying to lose my name these past two months or so.'

Dinakar smiled in a beguiling manner. With what effortless intimacy he spoke. His words seemed to Shastri like a sudden gift of grace.

'For your sake, I will return to my name. If you like, I will even return to the pet name that Mother gave me.'

This time, Dinakar spoke as if making fun of himself—he had made this part of his engaging TV manner—and then continued with some seriousness, 'Achcha, I need help from you. Twenty-five years ago, in Hardwar, I got acquainted with someone from Mangalore. I hear he is now a famous advocate. For a whole long month, we were close friends. This was also because of his mother—her name is Sitamma—the only person I ever felt was like my true mother. If Amma is still living, I want to meet her again.'

Taking from his bag an old address book, Dinakar showed Shastri the address of one Narayan Tantri. The sign that his whole life would change became stronger, and again in anguish Shastri forced himself to return to his everyday personality. 'Ayyo! These people are very dear to me, I know them very well. I always stop for a day at their place on the way to my village. Your friend's mother is still there. Every time I go, she makes me recite from a Purana. In these ten or fifteen years, I must have recited the same Purana many times to her. I myself will take you to them. This train reaches Bangalore in the evening and then at night there is a luxury bus to Mangalore.' Shastri surprised himself with his own volubility.

As he used his Bombay Hindi to speak of his present calling, Shastri remembered that he had learnt that language half a century ago, when he used to wear a shirt and pyjamas and a black cap to hide his brahmin tuft, with no caste mark on his forehead, while wandering like a lost spirit on the streets of Bombay. Therefore he felt that it was not he who was speaking but the demon that had entered him. Yet Dinakar looked at him with such earnest hope that Shastri spoke on without holding himself back.

' "Putani" means a dear son. I have no children now. The one daughter I had, walked out of my house two years ago. It is all my fate. You could have been my son.'

When Shastri risked saying those words, Dinakar replied with unaffected courtesy.

'If you feel like calling a bearded bumpkin like me your son, what can I call you? Shall I call you Chikappa, or Dodappa, or Mama?'

Hearing Dinakar speak in this way, Shastri was so shaken that he felt himself drained and insubstantial, like a wraith. But Dinakar was cheerful and, when the man in jeans took his autograph book out from his briefcase, he scrawled in Hindi, 'Not from the Dinakar of TV, but rather an ignorant putani who is now reaching Bangalore.'

Then, looking at Shastri, who had become pale, Dinakar spoke as sweetly as a putani. 'Chikappa, your Hindi sounds good to me. But please don't address me in the plural.'

Shastri kept staring at the amulet around Dinakar's neck, and what Dinakar now said in explanation made him even more fearful.

'Look, Chikappa, this amulet was tied around my neck before my mother went into the river Ganga. She never came back again. The food you fed me made me remember what happened. For forty years I have worn this amulet as matra-raksha.'

Hearing this, Shastri closed his eyes, grasped his rudraksha beads and silently prayed, 'Shiva, Shiva, protect me.'

3

Shastri was stupefied, as if he had been stricken. The language embellished for the pleasure of others which he had cultivated for recitation of the Puranas; the lewd language which he had learned in Bombay as if in a previous birth—neither çould express what he was beginning to understand in his anxiety. Dinakar was insisting that he accept a ride in his hired car to Mangalore.

'Look, Chikappa. Although I may be an Ayyappa bhakta, still I have a credit card.'

'Ayyo, it is not a question of expense. It is not safe to travel in the Ghat section during the night. I myself have plenty of money. I earn not less than

five lakhs of rupees from growing areca. And have
I children or grandchildren to spend it on? Why
then should I bother about money, why bother
about expenses? No, in order to work off my
karma, I have cultivated this addiction. I keep on
wandering, keep on doing what I do.'

Speaking these words with effort, Shastri found
himself desiring to address Dinakar as Putani, his
dear child, but the endearment stuck in his throat.
'What if he is the son of Pundit, what if he is that
prostitute's son?'

*

The taxi shared by Shastri and Dinakar wove this
way and that, through narrow lanes, climbing up
and down, and finally stopped in front of the
bungalow of 'Narayan Tantri, Advocate'. Dinakar,
whose eyes had become jaded from living in Delhi,
was cheered at the sight of the Mangalore-tiled
roofs, the many tones of faded brick-coloured tiles,
the little porches jutting out from the faces of the
old houses.

'Don't tell them who I am, Chikappa. I would
like to see whether "Mother" will recognize me
after twenty-five years, especially dressed as I am
now. If Amma does recognize me, it will mean
that Dinakar has not yet become nameless.'

Dinakar had become very light-hearted.
Walking easily, the bag swinging from his shoulder,

he opened the gate. Green hedges, mango trees and coconut trees had half hidden an old bungalow to which winding paths led, as if the bungalow were playing hide-and-seek on its two acres of land.

Shastri, counting his rudraksha beads, followed Dinakar.

An old woman was standing in the veranda outside the house, her white hair neatly combed. The eyes in her wrinkled face caught the light of the pole lamp; they shone in expectation of discovering who the visitors were. If a person is thin, it is said, you cannot tell their age. Sitamma looked not very different from her Hardwar days. She had more wrinkles and more white hair, that was all. Her white sari and her wet hair knotted at the end showed that she had just finished her bath.

The rangoli box in her hand made plain why she stood in the veranda. That black stone box must be the one she had bought in Hardwar when, along with other pilgrims, she had come to stay in the dharamshala built by Tripathi, Dinakar's foster father. Within a couple of days, the lustre in Sitamma's face had endeared her to Tripathi, and she had come to stay in their house. Every day she would get up at dawn, sweep and sprinkle the veranda, and after a bath in the river Ganga, she would spread her hair on her back. Then, with great concentration, she would take up pinches of different-coloured rangoli powder and, slowly sifting it between two fingers, draw on the earth of the veranda. So the ancient house of Tripathi suddenly acquired the charm of new prosperity. Sitamma had taken the vow of cooking for herself, and she insisted on doing all of the cooking. When the rangoli-laying was over, she would go into the kitchen to make upma or kesaribath or idlis, and feed everyone in the house as if she were their own mother.

She was at that time in her middle years, a widow of about forty-five. Tripathi was already seventy-five, a rich man from a good family, and a well-known charitable soul. With great affection, he would call Sitamma 'little sister.'

'Little sister, we too are brahmins, we don't even eat onions. You don't have to do all the cooking, you can eat what we eat.'

Since Tripathi spoke in Hindi, Sitamma couldn't understand him. But her son Narayan Tantri-had learnt Hindi in school as a result of the zeal of the Hindi movement, and also because he loved debates. Therefore, he became her constant interpreter.

*

Dinakar now stood before Sitamma and said 'Amma,' and Sitamma, with narrowed eyes, gazed at the amulet as Shastri had done. Then she looked into Dinakar's face. Her eyes slowly began to shine with the compassion of a mother and, as she went back in time, it seemed she was recreating him. Dinakar, in sweet pain, watched apprehensively.

'Ayyo, isn't it Dinakar?' she said. Because she was in a state of madi, having just bathed, she did not embrace him immediately. But her eyes gave him all the pleasure of a mother's touch. A moment passed like this. Then Sitamma turned to Shastri and said, 'What, Shastri-gale, why shouldn't I bathe again and then make your food?' So saying, she came and took Dinakar's hand, not even asking why he hadn't come to see her all these years. She cried out, 'Nagaveni, bring coffee!' Then, when she started to go inside to bring the rattan chairs out to the veranda, Dinakar said, 'Amma, lay your rangoli, I want to watch.' Although she didn't understand the words, Sitamma guessed his meaning.

'You always liked that, didn't you? Sit down. I will draw what you used to like in Hardwar. Watch while you drink your coffee. And you, Shastri-gale, go and have your bath. There is hot water if you want.' Smiling to herself, she squatted down to lay the rangoli.

With her thumb and index finger she took a pinch of rangoli powder and rubbed it to make it firm, moving her fingers just enough for the delicate thin line to appear. In a moment, at the very center of the swept and cleaned veranda, she had drawn two intersecting triangles, one upward-pointing and the other downward-pointing. In one, god's grace descended from heaven to earth; in the other, the soul ascended, aspiring toward God. Because of Sitamma's faultless eye, both met in perfect harmony.

Dinakar drank his aromatic coffee from a silver cup, becoming immersed in Sitamma's creation, as he used to do twenty-five years before. What for thousands of years took form on the walls of temples and in the verandas of cottages, no matter how poor, had begun to manifest this morning on the veranda swept with cow-dung. A vine where one was necessary, and a leaf on the vine; for every leaf a flower, and a swastika to guard it all, and then peacocks, and then—look—there was Lord Ganesha, and even his mouse to ride on.

As she drew the mouse, Sitamma smiled and said to herself, not bothering that Dinakar didn't understand Kannada, 'This has gone a little crooked. My fingers aren't strong enough. My hand shakes a little. Tomorrow I will do it better. Tomorrow Ganesha will come in the center. Tomorrow he won't be sitting, he will be dancing.'

4

'My Nani always gets up late. But his son Gopal is up very early. When we went to Hardwar, Gopal was a very small child. He had lost his mother. A girl called Gangubai used to look after him, you may remember her. She was crazy for getting bangles fitted, wherever she saw bangles she had to have them put on. Do you remember all this? She has a son now, younger than Gopal by a year. Gangu went to school again and has become a high school madam. Her child's name is Prasad. Our Nani got a house built for her. Gangubai got married from her mother's side. Her husband doesn't understand much, but he's a gentle one, like a cow. He also looks after cows himself, and he milks them. Some milk he keeps for the family, the rest he sells. You see?

'My grandson Gopal has begun to run about a lot these days. My son became president of this municipality—my big son did such great work—and now my grandson wants to save the whole nation. For appearance's sake he got "lawyer" put beside his name on the signboard along with his father's name. But does he care for his father's advice? Today he's in one party, tomorrow he is in another. Early morning he gets up and begins to phone while listening to Subbulakshmi's Venkatesha Stotra. You will see for yourself how he will buzz around when he sees you. Whenever we have seen you on TV we have talked about you. Nani says you must have forgotten us. But I always tell him, "I will not die before seeing him again." I say to Nani, "Why don't you write to him?" but Nani is lazy. "He has become a big man, he must have forgotten us years ago," says my son. What big man you are I don't know.'

As Dinakar sat on a stool in the kitchen listening to Sitamma, not understanding a word, she came to pinch his cheek—then remembered that she was in madi and laughed, stepped away, and squatted again before the earthen oven. She went on talking in the same way, waiting for the kadubu to be steamed.

Sitamma always cooked squatting at the firewood stove. She herself mixed the mud and built it, the main oven opening sideways into another, and then another. Every morning she would clean this stove, sweep it with cow-dung mixed with coal dust, and lay rangoli on it. Nobody else could arrange the pieces of firewood in the way she did, to make them burn with such a glow. In the main oven it would be bright and hot, and in the other two the flames would be diminished. On each one of these outlets Sitamma put whatever was the proper thing to cook there. She would sit before the stove and become as absorbed as when she was laying rangoli—here, lifting a little piece of wood to let fire catch in it, or pushing in or pulling out or placing one piece of wood on top of another, so that the fire would cooperate with another piece of fire, making the fire grow. Watching her skill in building the fire, Dinakar again remembered the Hardwar days.

In Hardwar she had got the right kind of mud and built a stove for Tripathi's house, and she who had come for ten days stayed for a month.

'What was I saying?' she said to herself, and kept on talking, even though Dinakar didn't understand.

'As soon as I saw the amulet, I knew it was you. Let us see whether Nani recognizes you in your new attire. And what about Gangu? But how could they forget you, they have even seen you on TV. How could they forget your eyes? If you had not taken this vrata, I would have waved drshti over you.'

Sitamma noticed Shastri at the kitchen door, listening intently as she spoke.

'Do you see how mad I am, Shastri-gale? How I am chattering away, forgetting that this boy doesn't know Kannada? In Tripathi's house, my belly felt as if on fire when I looked at this orphan boy. What a great man Tripathi was. He didn't let this boy down. Only five years old, they say, when his mother came to Tripathi's house, herself like an orphan. She came with a trunk and a bag full of clothes. Tripathi knew only that she was from the South. He was such a large-hearted man. Seeing what state she was in, he didn't ask, "Who are you? What about you? Why did you come?" and all that. He just gave her a place to cook her food and stay. He got her all the materials for setting up a kitchen. Just one time he asked her, because of the kumkum on her forehead, "Shall I go and search for your husband?" But when she stood there, not answering, her eyes full of tears, he never asked that question again. He even warned the other women not to ask her any such questions. Isn't one woman always curious about another?'

Seeing Shastri growing pale, Sitamma asked, 'Aren't you well? Didn't you sleep last night?' and she gave him a wooden plank so he could sit in the kitchen.

'Some five or six months passed like this. Then, I am told, early one morning the boy's mother got up and went to Tripathi. He was meditating in his puja room. This boy's mother was said to be a very graceful woman. Her eyes were exactly like the boy's. She wore the marriage-thread around her neck as well as this amulet. Tripathi told me all this, you see?—I started wanting to say something but I am telling you something else now—this boy's mother set down her trunk before Tripathi, touched his feet, and opened the lid of the trunk.

'Tripathi couldn't believe his eyes. There were at least two maunds of gold. A necklace, ear studs, bangles, and a gold belt. Not only that, there were also bars of gold. Tripathi showed it all to me. He guarded that trunk like a cobra.

'Think of my son as your grandson, and think of me as your daughter,' Dinakar's mother said, bowing down to God and then to Tripathi. Tripathi touched her head, blessing her, and locked the trunk in his iron safe. Could my two eyes alone be enough to see all that gold? The ornaments were from the days of the Vijayanagar Empire. They were on top, and the bars of gold were below.

'A month passed after this happened, and Tripathi became attached to Dinakar. He was like a child of the house. Tripathi had him and his mother live in his house, got him educated with his own money. He never touched the gold. But that is another big story . . .

'One morning, Dinakar's mother went to bathe in the river Ganga, and she never came back. They found her corpse some distance away. People said she could have slipped into the river. But everyone in Tripathi's house wondered why she had put the amulet around her son's neck just before she went to bathe. Why did she wake her son so early that day, and give him milk to drink?'

Sitamma had begun to cry. Dinakar guessed whose story she was telling. Shastri, sitting with closed eyes, counted his beads.

'As soon as I saw the amulet, I knew that it contained a Sri Chakra and was from our parts. From which house is this boy, who is his father, why did his mother leave home with a little child? Shastri-gale, you may recite from the Purana, but only Veda Vyas could have written a story like Dinakar's. The whole country thinks this child has grown into a very intelligent man, but this man doesn't even know who is his mother, who is his father, which is his town, so perhaps he wants to believe that God himself is his mother and father and that is why he wears these kinds of clothes and goes wandering here and there.'

Then Sitamma looked over at Shastri and

became alarmed.

'What is it? What is wrong?' she said, and quickly brought him water to drink.

5

As he listened to Sitamma's words, Shastri felt as if two pairs of red eyes were staring at each other furiously in his head. At times his second wife, Mahadevi, had looked at him silently with just such hatred. And at times he had looked at her in the same way. Later, he would feel puzzled, wondering why such fury burned in him without any reason.

His daughter had looked at him with that kind of hatred when she left home. When he had heard that she was in love with somebody in college, he had felt that burning fury and had said words that should never have been spoken. She too had spoken terrible words to her father. 'Can I be the same person,' he had asked himself in wonder, 'who in reciting a Purana can describe Prahlad or Dhruva with such moving tenderness?'

He wanted to know, yet he felt as if he was always running away from himself. Would the amulet around Dinakar's neck stop this running away? Seeing it had somehow brought him face to face with the mysterious rage inside him. Suddenly realizing that both pairs of furious staring eyes were his own, he felt fresh terror and again tried to turn his mind somewhere else.

Then he said, 'Sitamma, keep Dinakar in your house for two days. When I come back I will take him to my house in the jungle. He has agreed to stay with me for a couple of days before going to Kerala. I will go now, I won't eat anyway, because it is Ekadashi.' Although urged not to leave, Shastri went, hired a taxi from the stand, directed it away from the proper road, and entered a forest in which was the ruined temple of a goddess whom he had chosen for special devotion. The taxi had to travel on a path fit only for bullock-carts. 'I'll give you twice the fare,' he had said in the tone of the local landlords, and so the driver agreed to venture on the narrow bullock-cart roads. Shastri stopped the taxi in a thick jungle. He told the driver, 'Wait for half an hour,' then he pushed his way through bushes, making a path for himself until he stood before the ruined shrine of Bhagavati.

Shastri had been paying two hundred and fifty rupees each month to a poor brahmin from a nearby village to come daily and light a lamp for Bhagavati. At one time he thought of building her a new temple, but had held back from doing so because he feared that the aura of the Devi would suffer if he interfered with the existing shrine. He believed this in spite of knowing that the Shastras allowed the rebuilding of a shrine once the proper rituals were performed. He believed that this very Bhagavati was the fierce goddess who presided over the eyes that were burning in his head.

About a year earlier, unable to stand the daily quarrels with his wife, he had made a vow to Bhagavati and then brought Mahadevi to this place. She had stood before Bhagavati and begun to stare as if in a trance. Then she gave such an intense shriek that it slashed the silence of the forest. Looking at Shastri with her piercing eyes, she started to babble. Her accusations terrified him. How could she know that he had killed his first wife by smashing her head with a wooden lid? Mahadevi roared that she had become the ghost of that wife, and would go on haunting him.

Mahadevi became Saroja herself. 'Oh butcher brahmin, you killed me by beating me on my head! And were you not about to kill your daughter by your second wife?'

Shastri closed his eyes before Bhagavati and said, 'Bhagavati, did you make Mahadevi say a lie? Why did you have me believe until now that I was a murderer? Is Dinakar my son or is he the son of that Malayali pundit? Give me a sign so that I may know the truth. Don't make me keep wandering like a wraith.'

But Shastri did not receive any sign, and the blood-red eyes in his head kept on staring in fury.

*

He made his way out of Bhagavati's forest to where he had left the taxi. Then he directed the driver to take him to another village, some ten miles from Udupi.

In that village, there was only one big house, the one that Shastri had got built. When Shastri was in this house, the burning eyes in his head got cooled. It was the house of his mistress, Radha.

*

In Shastri's family, his elder brother had hated him, and Shastri hated him too. That brother suffered from asthma, didn't have any children, and his wife had died.

Shastri's elder brother never married again. He begged Shastri to marry and save the family, but Shastri would not agree. He did not like living in a jungle, cultivating the garden, eating—all throughout the rainy season—jackfruit palya, or sambar made with cucumber. And he did not want to live under his miserly brother's control, every day hearing that asthmatic breathing. So, fifty years ago, he had taken his share of the property and gone to Bombay, where he began squandering money. He also opened a hotel, the Bhagavati Krupa. But although he owned the hotel, he had somebody else sitting at the cash counter. Shastri had no care for what he earned or what he spent.

Nobody who had known him in his Bombay days would now say, 'This is the same Shastri.' In Bombay he had taken to wearing pyjamas and a shirt, and with a cap on his head seemed transformed into a Sindhi or a Marwari, even though he hadn't had enough courage to cut off his brahmin tuft.

It was also in Bombay that Shastri developed a taste for women. Pimps became his friends. He got into the habit of playing cards the whole day. His eyes were always red from going without sleep. Constant smoking had given him a cough, and he began to worry that, like his brother, he would get asthma.

*

One day, in a rich prostitute's house, Shastri saw a young girl. She spoke both Kannada and Tulu, and was seventeen or eighteen years old. Shastri was twenty-five. A pimp dressed in silk dhotra, trying to look like a respectable householder, had recommended 'a fresh high-school girl of your own side,' and taken him to look her over.

Shastri learned that the girl had been enticed away from a poor family in a village not far from Shimoga.

He was surprised at the compassion he felt for her, although he was a libertine and full of crude sexual desires for women. The madam who had bought the girl could not be won over by three of the four upayas—sama, bheda, danda—so Shastri then used the fourth upaya—dana—and gave the madam four times the money that she had paid. He also gave the name Radha to the grateful girl, and took her to the Bhagavati Krupa, where he kept her in one of his rooms as his woman. He gave up cards and gambling and instead began to keep an eye on her.

When a telegram came saying that his brother was not keeping well, Shastri took Radha with him. He left her in a Mangalore hotel with someone he trusted, and went to the village. By then his relatives were waiting for him to do the funeral rites.

The mouth of his asthmatic brother, which had always been open for breathing, was now closed. There were flies around his short pointed nose, that nose he had often felt like smashing. Even seeing his brother's corpse did not bring tears to his eyes. They had spoken such cruel words to each other. Now, remembering this, it seemed to him that they were a cursed family. He had never enjoyed his mother's love, she had died giving birth to him. His father, in old age, had married another woman. This stepmother thought that she was cursed, being the wife of an old man, and she made it her aim in life to give pain to everyone. Finally, she died after getting bitten by a snake in the garden. The father died of dog-bite, and Shastri's brother's wife of pneumonia. Shastri's brother then lived alone, a miser who dug up every corner of the house searching for gold which might have been buried there by ancestors.

There was already a lot of wealth which had been bequeathed to them—a trunk full of gold which must have been looted by some ancestor during the fall of the Vijayanagar Empire. The brother, looking for more, first dug up the whole house, then began digging in the garden. One day while digging, he died.

Shastri now owned the entire property. After his brother's funeral rites he took out the trunk from the iron safe to satisfy himself that his brother had not squandered the gold, and he felt relieved. Then he brought his 'dear parrot' Radha from the hotel and had a small cottage built for her on the bank of a river near an areca-nut garden. Then, considering who could look after her safety, he remembered Radha saying that she had an aunt in Shimoga. This aunt's husband was a tailor. Radha's mother—who had been mistress to a rich man in Chennagiri—had grown old and unwanted, so Shastri brought the mother as well. He bought a tiled house for Radha's family, and set up a cloth shop in the town for the tailor.

Shastri had no neighbours of his own caste near his house and gardens in the forest. His relatives who lived at a distance acted distant as well. They would have to come when there was a funeral rite in the house. Apart from this, nobody wanted to be anywhere near his place, and so Shastri could carry on his relationship with Radha fearlessly and unabashedly. He also bought a cloth-topped Ford car and took to wearing a draped dhoti with a shirt over it, and pump shoes; he drove his car on the cart tracks. All these things separated him still more from his relatives.

Two years went by in this way. Radha began to tell him, 'I am anyhow your mistress, but you must also marry.' He had no child by Radha, and this worried him. 'Am I cursed to be without issue in this house as well?' he thought.

'It may be my fate to be without a child,' Radha had said. 'You should marry and see.' In this way she kept after him.

Shastri had never in his life met another spirit
like Radha. It was not that she was without desires,
but that all her desires were contained within the
limits of family life. If she could get coconut milk
for her gruel and, on top of that, mango pickle,
this was what made her happy. And Shastri, who
went around burning in anger, would always soften
before Radha, enchanted by the charming words
which came from her sweet mouth. Unable to say
no to her, and also curious to know whether he
could father a child, he went in search of a bride.

Nobody in those parts would give a girl to this
wealthy, cursed house. They would raise some
objection about the household and then refuse.
There was no family elder with whom Shastri was
close, someone who could go about arranging his
marriage. And who respects a man who goes on
his own to ask for a girl? But at last, Shastri came
to know of a girl in a poor family near
Chikmagalur. Wearing a gold-bordered shawl and
draped in a dhoti, with a turban on his head like
a Mysorean and kumkum on his forehead to make
him look like a proper, traditional person, Shastri
went to ask for a bride.

Having produced eight daughters and desiring
to get at least the first one married, the parents—
noting the prospective son-in-law's wealth, lineage,
his family, his horoscope—and showing no desire
to know any other detail about him, agreed to give

their daughter Saroja in marriage.

Saroja was a beautiful, classically-featured girl. With her large, heavenly, indifferent eyes, Saroja got married without ever saying what she wanted. In the beginning, it had made Shastri proud that she liked reading books, that she was good at reciting the Mahabharata. Radha too was pleased that the girl was educated.

Radha even attended the wedding. Dressed like goddess Gauri, she came in splendour, the only loving member of the bridegroom's party. Radha's relationship with the wealthy Shastri wasn't unknown to Saroja's parents, but they acted as if they didn't know. Their only concern was where to seat Radha for the wedding dinner. Radha, using all the savings from the garden Shastri had given her, had bought gifts for the bride: a sari, and coral-studded gold bangles made by the famous craftsmen of Mangalore. No one else on Shastri's side had taken such delight in this marriage. No one else had given a present. Saroja's father and mother, worn out by being parents to eight girls, were comforted by Radha's affectionate nature, by her wealth and her expensive gifts, and felt that their daughter didn't have to worry.

To all their close relations they could boast, 'My son-in-law has a car, and he has a hotel in Bombay. Someone looks after it and sends him cash every month. He owns hundreds of acres of areca-nut garden. What's best, my daughter has neither a mother-in-law nor a father-in-law. She can manage things exactly as she pleases.'

The house-entering ceremony was over, the bride's party went back. Shastri remembers clearly even now that his beautiful wife never lifted her face and looked at him. He came to understand this was not shyness but contempt. If he took her hand playfully, she would stand like a statue of stone. In his memory, her eyes never met his eyes but passed over him as if he did not exist.

Shastri chided her, beat her, but nothing he did could change Saroja's indifference. She slept by his side dutifully, allowed him to enter her, but no fruit came of their contact.

Five years passed in this way, without Saroja becoming pregnant. Radha had supplied many medicines. She even counselled Shastri how to win over his wife in bed. But whatever erotic play he attempted did not loosen Saroja. He repelled her, and when the sexual act was over she would go to the bathroom, pour water over her head, then come and lie down on the bed with wet hair. In order to let his rage escape, Shastri would drive his car to Radha's house in the middle of the night.

The surprising thing was that Saroja was friendly with Radha, although without any touch of intimacy. Radha was fond of books, and she would send to Saroja stories and novels which she

had read. In return, Saroja would send to Radha
books she had got from her mother's house. Radha
sent Saroja jasmine flowers which she had grown,
delicately woven in banana fibre. After first offering
them to Sharada, whom she worshipped, Saroja
would fix them in her braided hair.

Radha would make excuses to visit the house,
saying that she needed banana leaves, or rope, or
rangoli powder. She would bring beaten rice that
she herself had made, and tonde grown in her
garden. Saroja always welcomed her politely,
saying, 'Come in,' and would make her coffee. But
she spoke no more than was sufficient for the
occasion. The two did not address one another by
name. If Shastri was there when Radha came, he
would straightaway call the servant, go to his car,
and supervise the cleaning of it. If Radha stayed
for a long while, the car which had been driven in
the dusty village tracks would become so clean
and spotless that it shone like the statue of a god.

6

Meanwhile, something happened that would change Shastri's whole life. A Kannada-speaking Malayali whose name was Karunakara Pundit opened an ayurvedic shop in Udupi. He was almost as old as Shastri, but he had a moustache and beard, and these enhanced the glow on his face. He had not cut his hair, but wore it in a big tuft. On his forehead he had a large sandal-paste mark, and his face had a quality of equanimity. His car was a better one than Shastri's. His clothes and demeanour made him appear a man of fortune. His Hindi was better than Shastri's, and he even spoke English. He had knowledge of allopathic medicine, and also of Sanskrit. For him, Sanskrit was as easy as drinking water.

Shastri and Pundit became acquainted, proceeding from asking one another, 'Of what model is your car?' Finally, Shastri confidentially obtained some aphrodisiac preparations from Pundit. Their acquaintance grew, they became friends, and one day Shastri took Pundit home for a meal.

As soon as Pundit entered the house, he looked around, and then stood meditating. His gaze became more serious and contemplative and Shastri, worried, lit a cigarette and stood before him in humility. Then Shastri gestured for Karunakara Pundit to sit down on a modern sofa that Shastri had bought after his brother's death, when he became the master of the house. Again Pundit closed his eyes and began to do japa, touching with his thumb the joints of his fingers. Then he opened his eyes and said to Shastri, 'Don't feel bad if I tell you something. I have some knowledge of tantra and astrology, which I have received from the traditional learning of my family.'

Shastri's regard for him doubled. He said, respectfully, 'Yes, please speak . . .'

'There is an evil in this house. Don't misunderstand me. It is that in some bygone time a woman was murdered here. That is why there is no progeny, no peace, for those who live here now. Some lowly spirits hover over people living here. As soon as I came in, I felt two burning eyes open in my brain. And when two other eyes opened to stare back at them, I began to do japa.' Hearing this from Karunakara Pundit, Shastri was stunned.

'A tantric rite must take place in this house. It should be performed jointly by husband and wife. Towards the end of the rite, the lady of your house will have to sit naked and offer worship.' Karunakara Pundit spoke as if he were prescribing the manner in which to take a medicine.

Shastri sighed and asked, 'Will you arrange to get it done?' Karunakara Pundit agreed and, consulting the almanac, found an auspicious day for performing the ritual. 'It will have to be done secretly,' he said.

7

Everything was made ready for the ritual. Saroja's eyes, usually blank with indifference, became totally intent as soon as Karunakara Pundit, wearing his silk dhoti, began laying the mandala on the floor using rangoli powder, kumkum and turmeric. Piously, she made cotton wicks for him. She shelled a coconut. She brought oil in a polished bronze long-spouted jug. Shastri felt happy, thinking that these were all good omens.

A sprightliness appeared in Saroja which Shastri had never observed before. The uneven parting in her hair was made straight. She put on all her bridal ornaments. After the ritual, the coffee she prepared was just the right temperature, and had not lost its aroma. Now she did not make coffee by heating an old decoction. It seemed to Shastri as if she were gradually developing a respectful attachment for Karunakara Pundit.

Of the prescribed month's puja, fifteen days were over. As it happened, the ritual had begun after the purification bath marking the end of menstruation and the beginning of fertility. When Saroja menstruated again, Shastri would have to do the ritual alone. And after another purification bath she would, for the last three days, have to sit naked and do the rites.

According to Karunakara Pundit, this was how it had to be done, even if others might perform it in a different way. Shastri felt confident that Saroja, because of her reverence for Pundit, would agree to the last stage of the ritual.

During this whole time, Shastri was not to sleep with a woman. He obeyed Karunakara Pundit and didn't even visit Radha. Saroja went through her menstruation and the sacred bath, sat naked and did the rites.

Karunakara Pundit would not accept any money from Shastri. But he did consent to accept a rudraksha mala in gold, and silk clothes, and he blessed the couple. Touching Saroja's head, he said 'May you become a mother of ten children.'

Shastri, who was very pleased, told him, 'You

should come and go more often.' So Karunakara Pundit began coming and going more often. One evening when Shastri had gone to Radha's house, Pundit came and then waited for him.

Shastri said to Saroja, 'Tell Pundit that he should come in the morning, because I won't be here in the evenings.' After a couple of days, Shastri grew suspicious and asked, 'Has Pundit come?'

'Yes,' Saroja said with indifference, Pundit had come.

Shastri controlled his rising anger and with mocking politeness asked, 'You gave him coffee, of course?'

'Yes.'

'Didn't you tell him that I wouldn't be here in the evenings, that he should come in the morning?'

Shastri remembers again and again how Saroja didn't reply to him, but turned and went into the house. The manner in which she stepped across the broad high threshold, raising her leg in utter disregard, straight-backed, pulling the end of her sari tight around her proud long neck, all that created a fire in his heart. Shastri got in his car and drove to Udupi. With a smile, Karunakara Pundit welcomed Shastri's burning face.

'What, Shastri-gale, you insist that I should come, but when I come you are not there. Every day you disappear. But your wife treats me with great courtesy.'

Karunakara Pundit took a pinch of snuff, then continued in an intimate tone, 'Your wife didn't reply to me when I asked her whether you have changed your bed-chamber. Perhaps I shouldn't have asked that question when you were not there . . . But tell me, do you find that the house is more peaceful now?'

The charm of Pundit's words calmed Shastri's mind. Pundit went on, 'I have asked you this because whenever I come to your house I see an angry spirit hiding in some dark corner or other, lying in wait to get hold of you. It is no ordinary spirit, but a bloodthirsty one. So you must keep meditating on the mantra that I gave you.'

'I came to ask you not to come in the evening, but in the morning. I am rarely at home in the evening—I have another garden that I have to look after. There is some disease in the coconut grove.'

Shastri tried to say this in a friendly manner. Earlier, he had imagined that Pundit did not know of his relationship with Radha. Yet now he felt frightened because, if Pundit could hear a spirit hiding in a corner of the house, wouldn't he know everything?

'Do you see something red burning in your brain?' Pundit continued. 'If, by God's grace, everything goes well, you will feel cool eyes opening in your heart. Until then, you will never be free from the bloodthirsty spirit. Such spirits make you roar "me me me" and so there is no peace for you. Think of the blue sky, imagine yourself floating in it, and meditate. I have prayed to my ishtadevata that she should warn me if either you or your wife is in danger. You requested that I come in the morning, but that's not possible for me. I have my own vows to keep, and patients come to see me.' He took another pinch of snuff and said, 'Look here, I too have a weakness. As long as we live in the body, we are all human. Kama, krodha, moha, leave no one untouched.' Pundit laughed and gathered his dishevelled hair into a knot. Shastri remembers that he burned, seeing how attractive Pundit looked as he tied up his hair.

Feeling he was under a spell, Shastri wanted to shout, 'Don't come home when I am not there!' If only he could say this, Pundit's spell would be broken. But he could not make the words come out of his mouth. 'If this Pundit has such a spell on me, what about Saroja?' Worrying over this, he drove his car back to the village. 'Pundit looks like a great connoisseur, perhaps he eats some special thing to make his breath smell so intoxicating . . . and what sandal-paste does he put on his body?' he wondered.

As soon as he reached home, Shastri began to fidget, thinking 'Saroja cooks and serves my food, gives me coffee whenever I want, but without speaking or looking at me, and even when she does look, her eyes still seem to be gazing far away. But when she sits with a book, her eyes appear to fix on something. Then she seems so absorbed, it's as if she is communing with herself. When she is stringing jasmine flowers her teeth bite her lower lip and she smiles as if sweetly conversing with the stem of the flower. Sometimes she puts her hands on her hips and, gazing at the parijata tree, hums to herself. All these things she does when she thinks that I am not looking at her. Otherwise, she is like another ghost in this house.'

Shastri began to feel anguish whenever he prepared himself to sleep with Saroja. After lying by her side for a while and finding himself unable to do anything, he would get up and go to Radha. One night, telling himself that Pundit probably would not come, he went to Radha, who made him drink almond milk and advised him not to come to her house, but to sleep with his wife.

She tried to teach him ways of seduction by showing him what he should do around the thigh, around the yoni, how to set the scene to win over Saroja. Shastri felt very envious, thinking that some other man must have done all these things to Radha. 'It's not as if you have no such knowledge. Why should I have learned it from anyone else?' Trying to console him, she continued, 'Have you forgotten? What have you not done to me when you brought me to this house, and what have you not got me to do to you? It seems a wicked spirit has entered you and made you dull,' she laughed. Shastri was shocked to hear her speak about the spirit in the same words that Pundit had used.

The next day, wanting to test his suspicions, he went at his usual time in the evening to Radha, but waited until eleven o'clock before coming back home. Pundit's car was in front of his house. His heart began to pound heavily. He feared that he might murder two people that night.

Trembling, he pushed the door to his house. It was not bolted. 'What guts!' he thought, wondering in his rage at their boldness. His ears were ringing from the blood that was rushing into his head, and along with the ringing in his ears he heard the alap of music. 'The bastards must be going at their work together with the music on the radio,' he thought. His legs felt weak. The music was coming from the puja room where Pundit had conducted the ritual. He must have already made her naked there, telling her she would become sacred. Now the bastard must be giving her womb his gift of seed. Shastri groped his way to the door of the room. It was closed. He pushed it open.

Ten buds of light were burning in two brass oil-lamps. Between them sat Saroja, hair over her breast, one leg folded under her, playing on the tamboura. Although Shastri had pushed open the door noisily, her eyes remained closed. She kept on playing the tamboura brought from her mother's house as if his coming there was of no consequence at all. He knew that she had been taught music, but he had never heard her sing like this.

In front of her, Pundit was sitting in the lotus posture. Not looking at Shastri, yet aware that he had come, he signalled for Shastri to sit beside him. Pundit began to join the alap. Now his voice would merge with hers, continue where she stopped, and she would anticipate and join him again . . .

'Arrey, he's playing host to me in my own house!' Not knowing what to do, Shastri sat. Saroja finished singing, touched the tamboura to her eyes, and put it down. In the soft cool light of the oil-lamp, nothing was clearly visible. Shastri held his breath, feeling the red eyes hastening to open in his brain. At the same time, he thought, 'No, I would not be able to beat and kill either Pundit or Saroja. I have become impotent.'

When the music ended, Pundit said to Saroja, 'I will come tomorrow,' and left the room. Shastri heard him slip on his chappals. Then heard the sound of his car starting. Then the drag on the first gear, and then the silence of all sounds receding. And then, in the cowshed, the now-and-then sound of the cows' bells as they chewed. And then no other sound. He thought, 'There must be only ghosts now, silently walking back and forth on their turned-around feet.'

Saroja got up and, as if nothing had happened, went to the bedroom. Shastri collapsed where he sat, as if he had died and become a ghost.

Then a strange thing happened to him—a fearful sound arose in his closed mouth, as if he had become a cruel beast secretly wandering among the deep bushes of a thick jungle.

The sound he made was a long sound, going higher and higher, then falling and falling into silence, terrifying him even when silent . . . and then it began rising again. It was a moan, and it was the bellowing of a cruel animal.

No human animal could produce such a sound.

Shastri felt that his body was making a sound more terrible than the cruellest language, something like the empty husk of a language. Inside him now there swelled a huge prideful demon that could eat language, that would destroy the waves of alap created by Saroja's divine throat a little while ago. It was something that could destroy all beautiful and tender things, kill the earth's inborn urge for good, for what nurtures the roots of plants and trees, for what makes birds build nests for their young, for what gives insects the power to move. Moaning, full of the enormous malevolence inside him, he moved with long strides to his bedchamber. He lighted a lamp and looked down at Saroja as she was drifting into sleep.

Even demons could not have engaged in such a violent coupling. He tore the clothes off Saroja and fell on her, shrieking and moaning. The way in which he took her was meant to destroy the cold untouched core of her, that unearthly indifference which negated him. That she did not suffer like he suffered, that her eyes did not flare in anger, that she endured him as if all his tantrums were irrelevant—all this fed the demonic rage in him even more.

But he has wondered over the years whether at the last moment, somehow, she could have given way . . .

Now, getting down from the car at Radha's house, this is what came from nowhere into his mind.

8

It was a terrible moonless day. That day he killed Saroja. Or so he had thought for forty-five years, until he saw the amulet on Dinakar's neck. Pundit had begun to come every evening. He seemed to have no inhibitions on account of propriety. That he was teaching music to Saroja was some sort of excuse for him. Also, he was growing medicinal plants in Shastri's backyard, where there was a deep pit of red earth. Even after digging upto a man's height, there was still fertile red earth left in it. Pundit himself had dug some up and kept it at the edge of the pit. Every day he used it for planting his new medicinal plants. He had given

Saroja the job of watering the newly-arrived ones.

Shastri would even see her carrying red earth on an iron pan. But the great noise within him which had pierced him in his swollen fury had settled gradually to a tortured pitch, a quiet, tormented moan that stayed with him constantly, like a pulse-beat.

Then one evening, in the backyard, Pundit had his dhoti tied up around his waist and, as if no one else existed, was explaining to Saroja, 'This is the scent of Vishnu.' He stood close to her, giving off his fragrance. He had put the leaves and roots of the plant on her palm, crushed them, asked her to smell them, and helped her hand to her mouth so she could taste them. Even when Shastri came and stood in front of them like a devil, Pundit took no account of him. Seeing Pundit's straight hairy legs, Shastri's heart began to pound, his whole body reverberating and wailing like a tamboura.

He felt he was growing impotent. Sometimes he would get sexually aroused when Pundit sat in the puja room and joined his pitch to Saroja's, intensity growing wave after wave, the two bodies, male and female, joining in alap—and then he would go to Radha's house. But even with Radha he remained impotent. Radha had taken to lighting ghee-lamps for the gods, and she also prayed to a private spirit in which she believed. She prayed that Shastri should be blessed with a child, that the ghost which haunted his house should leave, and that Saroja should be liberated from her coldness and flower into womanliness—that her hostile womb should welcome Shastri's seed. Shastri knew all this.

'Tomorrow, tomorrow, tomorrow,' he would tell himself, 'I will denounce the evil enchanter, I will spit in his face,' and he built up courage talking to himself like that. But he became timid again, while that Pundit, with his hairy chest and hairy legs, grew like a great-striding Trivikram. Yet when he saw the two of them in the puja room, he would say to himself, 'let him go to hell and teach her music,' and abandon his resolve.

One night he came home very late and saw that Pundit had parked his car in Shastri's accustomed place and was sleeping in his office. And in the bedroom Saroja slept, looking peaceful and remote.

Shastri became excited, imagining how Pundit would have had Saroja—if he did—and then he woke her up and took her. After it was over, she went out, took a head-bath, and came back. That made Shastri want to kill her. Unable to sleep by her side, he went and lay down on a mat in the room where Pundit was asleep. All through the night he ground his teeth, thinking that he had become a ghost in his own house. He watched every small movement of Pundit's as he slept, spent the whole dark night in this way.

Saroja probably gave coffee to Pundit when he was still half asleep in the morning. The bedding on which he had slept was neatly folded. Saroja must have done that. By now Pundit must have reached Udupi, bathed, applied sandal-paste on his body, and begun meditating on the art of seduction.

At the back of Shastri's house was a big hill, and on the hill was a jungle with leopards. In front of his house was a large veranda. Half a mile away was his nearest orchard. He owned many other orchards, and he also owned paddy-fields. Even his workers did not like to come anywhere near his house. The manager who looked after his estates had a plain tiled house near the workers' quarters. Shastri now went to these hutments, sought out the manager to scold him for not sending the men to work, and then went to oversee his other estates.

He visited Radha's house, ate some bananas, and drank hot milk. When he said that he would eat the dosas which she had made, she laughed, saying, 'Such a thing is not permitted here.' Shastri, observing the way she guarded his orthodoxy, forced a smile, thinking that he had not yet completely become a wraith. When she saw him smile so disturbingly, Radha went to the puja room, adjusted the burning wick, made the light burn brighter, and prayed for protection.

Shastri didn't feel like eating more than he had eaten already. So he wandered here and there, then came home at about three o'clock in the afternoon. He saw a pariah in the veranda and scolded him, 'What work have you here? Go and graze the cattle.' The pariah bowed and said, 'Mother said she would give me the leftovers.' Just then, Saroja came out and gave the pariah the lunch she had cooked for Shastri.

Shastri, waiting for Pundit's arrival, became aware that he was wailing again inside. He sat in his office, looking for the wailing to intensify, and willed, 'Today should be the end.' He received an omen from a lizard on the wall. It was then that the big clock struck and drummed its four hours into his brain.

Suddenly, he heard the sound of retching in the bathroom. He went to look and Saroja was there, trying to vomit but unable to do so. His vision darkening, he intoned like a wraith, 'Have you become pregnant, whore?' Afterwards, he often recalled the way she moved her neck as she stood there, bent over: was it to bring out the vomit, or to say 'yes'? That day, he had thought she was saying yes. Then Saroja stood straight, took water from the pitcher, and washed out her mouth. And the way she stood in front of him!

'O you adulteress, have you become pregnant from that bastard Pundit?' The demon inside him began to wail and laugh grotesquely. Didn't Saroja then stand calmly, unmoved, the amulet lying on her left breast as both breasts heaved with her breathing?

'How could I have completely forgotten myself at that moment?' he wondered. 'Was it because I could never bear how her beautiful eyes looked at me with such indifference? Or did I imagine then that those eyes were saying, "Who are you, bastard, to ask me such a question?" Or did this bhava of mine cause itself to think so, in order to prepare itself for what was to follow?'

Shastri lifted the heavy wooden cover of the big brass pot that was kept for hot water. Saroja had put both her hands on her head and bent it, but it seemed to him that her gesture was not from fear or pleading for mercy. It was more like a cow shaking its head, struggling to free itself when you are about to untie its halter. Before realizing that he would do it, he had smashed her head three times with the wooden lid. He felt her blood splatter his face. Lifting her slumped body, he strode like a gloating demon on his two great legs, from the bathroom to the backyard. She had seemed dead, and he had thrown her into the red earth pit. Then he had come inside, wailing; had changed his clothes, thrown his blood-soaked clothes into the red earth pit on top of her, and driven away quickly in his car. 'Why didn't I suspect that Saroja might not have died? I had beaten her only at the back of her head,' he thought. But then he realized that if such an idea had come to him, he would have beaten her further and made sure to kill her.

*

'Soon Pundit will arrive, see what has happened, and inform the police,' Shastri thought. Then he decided he would kill Pundit too and throw him into the pit. After that, he would go to Kerala for a few days. So, although he had set out for Kasargod, he turned the car around and when he reached home again it was eight o'clock, with the oppressive darkness of a moonless night. In his frenzy he had left without locking the door, and when he entered the house it seemed frighteningly silent. Had Pundit already come and gone? Or was he about to come just now? Fearfully, Shastri made his way in the dark to the pit, took a hoe, and dragged all the dug-up earth back into the hole. Breathing heavily, he worked for an hour. 'Tomorrow morning I will get up, level this place, and plant a jackfruit sapling there,' he told himself. He sat on the steps of his house with a sickle in hand, waiting to kill Pundit. But Pundit did not come. 'Arrey, has the enchanter come and gone? Has he already complained to the police?' Without sleeping, Shastri waited. But nobody came.

In the morning he added more earth and levelled the pit. Then he left, this time not forgetting to lock the door. He drove to Mangalore and stayed in a hotel. After two days of fearful waiting, surprised that he was still safe, he returned home.

The red earth pit was just as he had left it. But in front of the house there were tyre marks from Pundit's car. 'Were those marks left behind by Pundit after I killed her and drove away in my car?' he wondered. Then he went into the puja room and saw the door of the iron safe standing open. The trunk full of gold was gone. All at once, the horror of having done murder vanished in the rage against Pundit that began to howl in him.

'O the enchanter robbed me and ran away! His eyes were not on Saroja, but on gold. Yet he even made her pregnant.' Calculating, considering whether he should report to the police that Pundit had killed Saroja and run off with the gold, Shastri drove to Udupi and stopped the car in front of Pundit's shop.

Pundit's door was locked. Shastri, widening his bloodshot eyes, asked the neighbouring shop owner, 'Where is he?'

'Ah, yes. One evening, it must have been three days ago, yes, on the new moon day—Wednesday evening—he left and has not returned since. I thought he had perhaps gone to your house.' Did the shop owner Kamath smile falsely, as if there were some hidden meaning in his words?

'No, he's a householder like me,' Shastri told himself. 'He is my age, has children, and he even keeps a lorry.' Shastri felt fully reassured that Kamath did not see him as a murderer but only as a customer when Kamath said, 'I have got excellent toor dal from Hyderabad, only one bag left. Shall I have it put in your car?'

Refusing the dal, Shastri had gone to Radha's house. He had not seen her for some days. She touched his forehead and said, 'Ayyo, you are feverish.' She opened a bedroll and made him rest on it, and for the first time ever he told her a lie.

'That useless one ran away with Pundit three days ago. The whore also took the trunk of gold.' His scheming mind had decided not to complain to the police and risk getting into a criminal suit.

He went back home, took more earth from the paddy-field, and added it to the pit. In the center of the pit, he planted a jackfruit sapling. He told people that the fruit would be as sweet as honey, and people were surprised at the unfamiliar friendliness in Shastri's hostile, ever-burning face.

9

Shastri got down from his taxi and asked the driver, who was whistling away merrily, to wait. He went into Radha's house with his bag.

'Look, here is a Madras sari for you,' he told her. Although Radha was pleased, she knew there was something else on his mind. 'What is the matter?' she asked. Shastri was surprised by the relief he felt when he found himself replying, 'I believed I had told you a lie. But after forty-five years, I see that what I told you may be true.' Then, in great detail, he explained to her his present state of uncertainty.

'I had last seen the amulet on Saroja's neck

when I was in a state of utter fury. When I saw it yesterday, it seemed to me a sign that I could die and be born again.'

'But how can I say whether he is my son or Pundit's? When Mahadevi had a daughter from me, I realized that Saroja too might have been pregnant from me. Then I feared that I would rot eternally in hell for killing not only Saroja but my own child, so I began to work off my life in this new costume of reciter of Puranas. Yet it seemed this body into which the demon had entered has never learned anything. Had I not felt that very same kind of rage towards my own daughter? I might have killed her, but she escaped. Now Mahadevi feels rage like that, and wants to kill me. And I feel the same. But am I, speaking to you now like this, the same person who felt my heart turn over as I watched someone who might be my son eating the food I gave him?'

Shastri's throat choked with emotion. But then he chided himself, 'I should not seek sympathy from Radha so that I neglect to observe my own hell.'

He looked at Radha, waiting for her reply.

'I have not told you this,' she said. 'The servants here always gossiped that you killed your wife and buried her in the pit. They say that is why the jackfruit tree you planted there does not bear any fruit. I didn't tell you lest it would give you pain.'

Radha sighed, adding, 'God has saved you.' She went inside and brought milk and fruits, then sat down and pressed his feet. But Shastri drew his feet back.

'Do you think Pundit lifted her from the pit, when she was half-dead, and then took the gold from the safe? Yet it doesn't seem he was a thief . . . when she was washed away in the river, all the gold she had brought with her was still untouched. But then why did he leave her? Or did he die, and did she take refuge in Tripathi's house because she was alone? She must have lived with Pundit at least until her son was five years old. And I heard that she had kumkum on her forehead when she went to Tripathi's house, so she didn't go as a widow.'

He fell silent for awhile.

'I don't want to care whose son he is, yet that is how I feel. Couldn't he be Pundit's son? But then, I might have created him when I was howling like a demon. Now I am sure of nothing. Was it really Saroja herself who went to Tripathi for shelter, or could it have been someone who resembled her?' Shastri began to pray, 'O God, save me from these tormenting doubts which make me like a ghost in limbo.'

Radha came, sat by his side, held his hand tenderly, and said, 'Believe that he is your son.'

'One moment I believe so, but the next moment

I think that Pundit made him, and I feel fire burning in my stomach.' He got up without drinking any of the milk she had brought him.

When Radha asked why, he said, 'Hereafter on Ekadashi I will not even drink milk.'

10

Radha saw signs of Shastri's release from the demon which tormented him. For a whole year she had been holding onto a secret, something which was essential for his liberation. Now she watched him, hoping that in a few days she could reveal to him what she knew.

Shastri looked at Radha's hair, which had begun to turn gray, and her lovely, still-unwrinkled face, which glowed with warm affection.

'Why did I ever marry Mahadevi? Of course, you were urging me to marry. And I thought that if I had a child my troubles would go, and I would have peace. Saroja tortured me with her beauty

and indifference. But Mahadevi was just like me.
From the start she fell on me with her eyes burning.
She is nothing like Saroja. She hates you too. And
my daughter is truly my daughter. Stubborn.
Marrying an idiot who wants to make revolution
and destroy people like me with good family
backgrounds. She left my house, I don't know
where she went. Sometimes I feel a desire to bring
her back home. Who knows what I become from
moment to moment? Perhaps for people like me
there is no release from this bhava, we stay
entangled in this world. But at least Saroja has not
died by my hand. I prayed to God to be released
from bhava because, when my daughter was born,
I suffered thinking that Saroja could have become
pregnant from me. What God can give me solace?
My fate is written here,' he said, touching his
forehead, suddenly feeling as if he were speaking
well-rehearsed words in his role as puranik.

He returned to the waiting taxi and went home.
He did not expect that as soon as he entered the
house, Mahadevi would pounce on him without
any reason. But, seeing her standing before him as
if to devour him, seeing her flared nostrils in a
contorted face, he felt, to his surprise, compassion
welling in him for this helpless woman.

Mahadevi at once started to pick a quarrel over
Radha's wealth and the gold bangles Radha had
got made for a grandchild. She kept saying,

'Because of your murderous nature . . .,' working herself into a fury and screaming about the daughter she had lost. Shastri had never before touched Mahadevi in consolation. But now he embraced her although she tried to squirm away, probably thinking that he was going to strike her. But instead, very gently, he spoke her name over and over, 'Mahadevi, Mahadevi . . .'

'I have not killed anyone, Mahadevi. What the servants said was wrong. I myself once believed as they did. But yesterday in the train I came to know the truth.'

He knew that Mahadevi couldn't make sense of all he said. But, feeling the tenderness of his touch, she wept, and he caressed her and said, 'Don't cry. I will find out where our daughter is and bring her here.'

Looking surprised, Mahadevi went inside the house, blowing her nose with the end of her sari. Shastri felt a faint hope that he might be healing. He looked at the parijata tree growing haphazardly in front of his house, the crooked-in-eight-ways tree which, by shedding on the earth all its delicate blossoms, fulfills itself. Saroja used to gather its flowers with the tips of her nails, careful not to wither them from the warmth of her fingers. One by one she would pick them up, collect them in a banana-leaf cup, and pour them over the snake pit which had formed in the backyard. Remembering this, Shastri again felt pain. Why had there been kumkum on Saroja's forehead when she was carried off in the river? Why was there a marriage thread around her neck? Had it meant that Pundit was not dead? Or did it mean that the one who had held her hand in marriage was not dead?

Feeling weak, the fragile signs of his recovery fading, he went into a bathing-room. It was not the same bathing-room in which he had smashed Saroja's head. That one he had got torn down, and he'd had another one built in a new place.

BOOK TWO

BOOK TWO

11

First, as if from the depths of a cave, one, one, or two, two, sprouts of melody, and now the clear sound of a bell emerging, and then a bass melody oooooo, and then jingling as if from belled anklets. All melody as if made from itself inside itself. As if going deeper and deeper down inside, melody wandering and searching the depth of the depths. Even as everything ended, again a melody arising from a deeper side of the kundalini. Did the melody find what it sought? As if saying look, look, the wonderment of small, small bells. Was it being lost, or drowning in ecstasy?

*

Dinakar, reading an English translation of *Bardo Thodol*, listening on his Walkman to the chanting of Tibetan lamas, tried to relate his present state of mind to the bardo state described in *The Tibetan Book of the Dead*. Not reclining on a pillow, he sat up straight on a mat.

He was in the drawing room of Narayan Tantri's big house, sitting straight-backed even though mattresses were laid out together with large cushions covered in white cloth. Sitamma saw Dinakar and said, 'What has happened? Come sit on a mattress.'

She saw Dinakar smile and said, 'Ayyo, I keep forgetting that you don't understand Kannada. Get up and take a bath. Then I will give you your morning food. Everyone will be awake very soon. As soon as he sees you, my grandson will start dancing about and troubling you. That's why I haven't told him you have come, I left him tied to his phone. Get up, get up!' Then she made gestures to make clear that he should take a bath.

Dinakar took a clean towel and Pears soap from her, surprised that after twenty-five years she still remembered he was fond of Pears. Humorously, forgetting that Sitamma wouldn't understand him, he said in Hindi, 'This means you are my other mother.' Sitamma shot back, 'What? Early morning you get up and right away you speak to me in the Sahib's tongue?'

She went on, 'Tripathi was such an orthodox brahmin, my dull mind could never understand why he spoke that Sahib's language.' Then, feeling shy that perhaps she had said something which she ought not to have said, she covered her mouth with the end of her sari and, laughing, entered the kitchen.

By the time Dinakar came out of his bath, all was festivity.

Gopal, Narayan Tantri's son, flung himself at Dinakar's feet and then began dancing about. 'See,' Sitamma said, 'my grandson will boast of you to his whole gang and get his dinner out of it as well.' As Sitamma stood making fun like this, Narayan Tantri caught his mother's eye and gestured that she should not embarrass Dinakar. Dinakar considered the changes in Narayan Tantri. 'I would certainly not have recognized him. He has grown stout. And now he weighs his words like a public man.' The sharpness and mischievousness of his old friend didn't seem to be there. Dinakar felt a little disappointed to think that he had found a mother again, but not a brother.

As he watched Narayan Tantri, Dinakar's resolve to confide in him withered. How could he speak to this successful public man of the secret that gnawed at him?

He had even prepared what he would say to his friend.

'Look, Narayan, it seemed there was nothing sacred left in my life, so I began wearing these clothes. After my foster father died, his sons had become very greedy, and I went less and less often to their house. Their eyes were on the gold which Tripathi had never even touched. I felt disgusted, but gave them what they wanted. Now I go there only for Tripathi's shraddha.

'After my education in England, I lived in Delhi. Slowly I became empty. I could say anything, charm anyone. I didn't know where my roots were. Even if I searched for them, I knew I could not find them. But it wasn't in my nature to be lonely, either, and I lived a dissolute life. The women I made love to then are everywhere now. In Lucknow, Delhi, England—but gradually I got tired of this. Trying to hide one woman from another, having affairs . . . the weariness increased. At the same time, it was an addiction.

'All this business began in Hardwar, in my twentieth year, when I was with you. Even while I felt that I was being reborn—that, having lost my mother, I was reborn in your mother—even in those days I kept a big secret, without any regret, and I was happy with that secret. But now I want to understand what happened to me then.'

Such words went round and round in Dinakar's head as he tried to bring himself to speak of what was so important to him. Hopelessly, Dinakar looked at his old friend. Meanwhile, Narayan Tantri was flattering Dinakar with elaborate hospitality. Perhaps, Dinakar thought, his friend had also prepared for himself a voice meant to obscure some hidden sorrow.

12

Banana leaves cured on the hot ash of the bathing-room fire. On these fragrant, bud-shaped banana leaves, kadabu steamed in cups made of jackfruit leaves, and on the kadabu, yellow-coloured ghee from cow's milk. Three different types of chutneys. In a banana cup, creamy curd. On the side, hot steaming coffee.

Dinakar, who didn't know the Kannada names of any of these foods, sat and ate with great appetite. Narayan Tantri and his son Gopal had bathed and, sitting by Dinakar's side, ate more than he did. It was Sunday, the courts weren't in session, and Narayan Tantri seemed more relaxed.

But although Gopal ate his food, he was eager to go and share news of Dinakar's arrival with his cronies.

There was a sound from the backyard— somebody calling out 'Amma.'

'Who is it? Chandrappa? Just stay and wait a little,' Sitamma said, going into the yard.

She came in again, ladled some kadabu and chutney onto a banana leaf, and on her way to the backyard said to her son, 'Gangubai wants to meet you. Chandrappa has come to ask whether you will be at home. I told him, "Let Gangubai come." ' Then she took the leaf-plate out to Chandrappa.

Sitamma, who was very fastidious about eating taboos, didn't serve Chandrappa or Gangubai or Prasad inside the dining room. But she would never let them go without giving them something to eat and exchanging courtesies, inquiring after their joys and sorrows.

Gopal seemed displeased that his grandmother had invited Gangubai home, and Narayan Tantri's face fell when he observed his son's angry look. Dinakar could not quite make out what was happening between father and son, but he remembered that Gopal had been a very obstinate child, and that when Gangubai was a girl looking after him, she often resorted to the four upayas to get him to sleep. Sitamma took no account of the tension of the moment, but went to the backyard and began to talk of this and that with the dull-witted Chandrappa.

'How much milk does the cow give? Has the white cow become pregnant? Were you able to sell the male calves? How much did you get for them? How long is the school holiday for Gangubai? Why doesn't Prasad show his face here at all? How is his music going? How well he sang in the temple on Ramnavami.' Sitamma had already asked most of these questions many times that week. As usual, she expected no answer from Chandrappa. Her only aim was to make him happy.

Chandrappa looked at her, listening to her affectionate words with his mouth slightly open. Seeing his open mouth, Sitamma said, 'What, isn't the kadabu tasty? Shall I bring some more curd? It is the curd of Tunga, your own cow, so thick you have to cut it with a knife.' This Chandrappa understood. He shook his head, said, 'No, Mother,' and began to eat the kadabu.

Sitamma, seeing a coconut which had fallen from a tree in the backyard, brought it and said, 'Chandrappa, will you please shell this for me?' There was no need for it to be shelled, but she knew that Chandrappa delighted in any manual job, especially where he could use a knife. In his house, it was he who cleaned Prasad's bicycle so that it shone without a speck of dust, then oiled it and tied a garland of marigolds on the handlebars.

On festive days, it was he who brought mango leaves and festooned the door with them.

When Sitamma came back into the house, she looked angrily at Gopal. She knew what he was waiting to say. Gopal spoke with a heavy face. 'Let Father go to her, if he wants. But she should not come here. You must know how the whole town talks . . .'

'Can you or anyone stop wagging tongues? Who are they to us? Let your politics go to hell! I know your worry is only that the brahmins here won't vote for you. Just think, your mother died immediately after giving birth to you and didn't even see you, do you know that? It was Gangu who carried you about and played with you. Get up, go, bow down to God and ask forgiveness for your bad thoughts. Take this rupee and put it in the box for the god of Tirupati.' From the coins tucked in her waistband she gave him a rupee. She had many coins left there, for the beggars who came to the house.

Gopal took the money from her like a little boy and, with a sigh, walked to the puja room.

Sitamma sighed too. With relief.

13

As Gangu came down the stairs after finishing her talk with Narayan Tantri, she seemed to be in tears. Narayan Tantri followed, looking down as he descended the steep, old-fashioned stairs, holding onto the railings so as not to lose his balance.

Even after twenty-five years, Dinakar's heart pounded at the sight of Gangu. Still slim, with her salt-and-pepper hair in a bun, her pallu pulled around her shoulders and held with both hands, Gangu looked a mature, handsome woman. She came downstairs without any support, touched Dinakar's feet, and, in traditional welcome, said,

'Have you come?' She didn't seem to have lost her passion for bangles. The many she wore on both arms expertly harmonized with her sari and blouse.

Dinakar managed not to reveal his feelings because Sitamma came over and began to talk pleasantly. He noticed that Narayan, with hands clasped behind his back, was observing his reaction to Gangu. Dinakar reflected that his sexual impulses had not changed in spite of the Ayyappa clothes he now wore. Feeling awkward, yet wanting to say something for the sake of propriety, he began making small talk in Hindi.

Even in the old days Gangu knew Hindi, which she had learnt in high school. She used to speak with such playfulness, but now she stood quietly, listening to Sitamma who was saying, 'Our Gangu is not an ordinary person. Can you say that she has aged? Doesn't she look as she did in Hardwar? I tell her, "Dye your hair just a little, here and there," but she has got vairagya in her. She has become a madam after finishing college. Whenever she comes back from school, she has a bunch of children following her. She is truly a kindari jogi. But can one say that only she has vairagya? Her son also has vairagya. He is like sage Shukamuni. Not at all like our Gopal, the jewel of our family. Gangu's son doesn't even wear a shirt, he puts on a white dhoti and white upper cloth, and sports a long beard. You should hear his singing, when he

is singing it seems as if Tyagaraja was born again.
Our Gangu is truly blessed.'

Gangu looked pleased by what Sitamma said.
And Dinakar was amazed at Sitamma. Even though
he couldn't understand the language she was
speaking, he could see how her words made
everyone happy.

14

'The beach near Suratkal is beautiful. Let's go there,' Narayan said to Dinakar as soon as it was evening. Narayan drove his car himself, but his thoughts seemed to be elsewhere. Dinakar suspected that Narayan, like himself, was waiting to say something. But Narayan talked on and on, full of praise for Dinakar's TV show about the election, his report on South Africa, his various articles, and so forth.

Dinakar walked on the clean pure sand of the beach, looking with pleasure at the sea which rose in waves, approaching and then receding, enjoying it in silence. Then Narayan turned to him, held his hands, and said, 'I must tell you something. I have wanted to say it all these twenty-five years, but was unwilling to speak. I had even thought it might be better not to meet you. When I saw you today, I thought, "Why on earth did he come?" But after seeing Gangu this morning, I decided that I must tell you.' Then he stopped.

For a while, both men stood gazing at the sea, not saying anything. The setting sun bathed the whole sky in colours that changed every moment. There was no one else on the beach except for a few fishermen who were spreading their nets. Dinakar sat on the sand, began pushing it into small mounds, and waited.

Although he was a man of forty-five years, Dinakar felt himself becoming a boy again. He could hear anything, say anything. And Narayan seemed free from the English which in public he used so carefully. Now he unthinkingly mixed in Kannada words, speaking as if talking to himself. Yet Dinakar had not brought himself to say what he wanted to say. He thought that he should speak out, yet he was reluctant to interfere in Narayan's inner conflict. The sky was becoming bare, losing its colours, returning to its own true state as it had done from time eternal.

'Dinakar,' Narayan began, 'you know after my wife died I didn't marry again. Gangu came as a maid servant and became part of the family. She brought up Gopal. Back then, she had been married off to someone on her mother's side. Her mother had belonged to the prostitutes' community. As was the practice, for the sake of appearance, she had given Gangu in marriage. The husband was one of her own dull-witted cousins—the man who came this morning to our house. The fellow is as gentle as a cow and he actually lives by tending cows. Gangu hadn't wanted to follow the profession of her mother, so she came to our house. She had by then finished her high school. After coming back from Hardwar, I put her in a college. Her mother, who had always been after her, had died, so Gangu felt free to do what she liked.'

Narayan stopped talking. Dinakar, who had been digging the sand, began to take out wet handfuls, and shaped them into shivalingas. He remained silent, certain now that he could never tell Narayan what he wanted to say. Narayan began speaking again.

'You did not know that I had a sexual relationship with her in Hardwar. And I did not know that you had a relationship with her.'

Dinakar suddenly felt very light. For a moment he wanted to say, 'But I possessed her first, when she was still a virgin.' Then, ashamed of his crude impulse, he quietly went on listening to Narayan.

'Only a few days later, after we came back

from Hardwar and she began college, did I come to know she was pregnant. I was scared, though also relieved knowing that people would assume the child belonged to her husband . . . I am by nature a practical man. Gangu insisted that she should have an abortion, otherwise it would be difficult for her to study. Although I thought the same, I felt I should say, "No, have the child." After she became pregnant, Gangu began to love me so much that I developed an attachment for her which I never had for my own wife. The way she felt helpless made me love her more. I bought a house for her, and saw to it that there was a little garden and a cowshed at the back. My mother also pressed me about this. What I bought then for half a lakh would now cost at least twenty lakhs. Land prices in Mangalore have become like Bombay.

'Never mind. Gangu was four or five months gone in pregnancy, the baby inside her had begun to kick, and again she kept after me that she wanted to abort. Then one night, as I was lying beside her, she began to sob and tell me of the affair between you and her. "I don't know whether this child is yours, it could just as well be his," she said. "Leave me if you don't like me," she said, and kept on sobbing.

'A great rage against you and her arose in me, more for her than you. I wanted to beat and kill her. Maybe my lawyer's cautiousness held me back, or the merit of my ancestors. Never mind. I thought she must be an enchantress and I suffered, thinking about the power of this woman who could hide from me in Hardwar her love for you.

'I stopped seeing her for a few days, but then I went to her again. I couldn't check my desire for her. They say that when you lust, you have neither shame nor fear.

'I took her to Bangalore secretly and found a doctor willing to do the abortion. The night before the abortion, as she slept in a hotel room by my side, she herself looked like a child. I cannot explain what happened to me then. It must have been the doing of my god.

'Suddenly I thought, "What does it matter if the child is mine? What does it matter if it is Dinakar's? It is still a child that is floating and growing in her womb. Let it be born and let it grow. I will believe that it is mine."

'When I thought all this, I woke Gangu and told her. She embraced me, weeping with joy. The next day I brought her back from Bangalore. Who knows what Mother felt when she saw me? She scolded me, "You have not worshipped God in so many days. Take a bath, then go to the puja room."

'I believe there must be something of my mother's grace in the change that took place in me.'

15

In the sky, the sun's love-play was over and the moon's grace appeared. While the sky seemed serene and peaceful, frothing waves moved over the sea, like thousands of white horses rushing forward in battle. The waves wet the feet of the two friends. Dinakar got up first. Then Narayan, who seemed to have been in deep meditation, lifted his heavy body by bracing his hands against the sand. The rudraksha beads on Narayan's neck caught Dinakar's attention, and Narayan Tantri in turn looked at the amulet on Dinakar's neck.

'You've always worn that, haven't you?' Narayan Tantri said.

Dinakar felt eased of tension by this casual question, although he was still aware of the profound effect that Narayan's earlier revelation had created.

'That is matra-raksha,' Dinakar said. 'My mother hugged me and tied it around my neck before she went to bathe in the river. Inside me there is a painful knot of unanswered questions. Did she tie the amulet around my neck knowing she was going to kill herself, or did she accidentally fall and die? Who is my father? They say my mother wore a tali around her neck and kumkum on her forehead. That means she was not a widow, she must have left my father. But why did she leave him? And whose gold was in the trunk? My father's? My mother's? That gold must be tainted . . . because of it my benefactor's children became greedy. It also led to the shamelessness of the woman I married.

'By today's reckoning, the gold must be worth a crore. Sometimes I am tormented, wondering "Did my mother steal it? Is it dirty gold?" But I feel lighter because I have lost half of it. That is another big story, I shouldn't go into it now,' said Dinakar. Then he went on to tell it just the same.

'You remember how Tripathi used to sit on that chair, a stick in his hand, kumkum on his forehead, neatly shaven, with a big white moustache, a gold-bordered shawl around his shoulders. Even now I can see him sitting there like a king. He had a very strong voice. He would sit on his chair and get everything done in his masterful way. Exactly the image of a feudal lord. Yet he was also a great philanthropist. Every day food was given to people in the dharamshala he got built. He never touched any of the gold from my mother's trunk. He educated me in English schools with his own money. But the son he had who was my age, he sent to a Sanskrit school, trying to bring him up as another Tripathi. From the beginning, that son didn't like me. When his father couldn't hear what he was saying, he would insult my mother and make me cry. He hated me because I was his father's favourite. So Tripathi himself bears some of the fault. A man who looked after everyone else with such lordly kindness did not treat his own son with enough kindness.

'Even before I went to Oxford, Tripathi's influence had begun to wane. His son stopped the daily feeding in the dharamshala. Tripathi would sit in that old chair of his, stick in hand, like an aged lion, and he grew increasingly more melancholy.

'Now I believe that Tripathi was perhaps an ichchamarani. One morning, after his dip in the Ganga, he could not sit up straight in his puja room, so he leaned on a wooden plank. Even though his own son knew Sanskrit and wore a tuft like him, he didn't call his son. He sent for me, with my modern cropped hair, and said, "If you have already bathed, put on your silk dhoti and come." I wore as an upper cloth the silk dhoti that he had given me in my eighth year, after my mother's death, when he whispered the Gayatri mantra into my ears and got the thread ceremony done. I put on the gold-bordered silk dhoti which he gave me the previous Navaratri, and sat before him. I have a good voice. People say that my mother was a good singer, and I must have got it from her. Tripathi requested me to recite the stotras composed by Adishankara. But before I started reciting, he asked me to bring the bunch of keys from his bag. From this big bunch of keys he took one out and gave it to me, saying, "I have kept your mother's gold in my small iron safe. Here is the key. Be careful, keep it from my greedy son. When you go to England, don't leave the key here. After you come back, as your gift for having grown up in this house, rebuild the temple which my ancestors had built on the bank of the Ganga. In England, don't eat what ought not to be eaten, don't drink what ought not to be drunk. Come back, then marry a girl from a good family and become a good householder." I fell at his feet and he blessed me.

'As I began to recite Shankara's stotras, he closed his eyes and never opened them again.

'I finished my studies in England, came back, and rebuilt the temple. His son did not particularly want this done. The dharamshala built by Tripathi was slowly becoming like a hotel. Those who came to stay there were now asked to pay some money in the form of a donation.

'They even had to pay for hot water.

'This saddened me deeply. Then, one day, Tripathi's son brought an accounts book and showed me some acccunts on old yellowed paper. I could tell he himself had written this, but he pretended that his father had done so. He forced a smile and told me, "Look, these must be expenses incurred by my father on your behalf."

'The account he placed before me was for nearly ten lakhs. I began to tremble in disgust. I went and got the trunk from the iron safe and told him, "Don't bring dishonour on your father's soul by yapping at me that this account was written by him. Just take from this trunk whatever you want." That made him unsure of himself. So I went and sold some bars of gold and gave him ten lakhs. Then I took my trunk with what remained in it, and came away to Delhi.'

*

When he realized that Narayan, walking by his side, was not responding, Dinakar felt ashamed. 'Have I acknowledged the nobility and sacrifice of his feeling "Gangu's son could be your son, but I will bring him up as my own?" Is it right for me to be boasting of my generosity in giving away gold?' Dinakar felt dismayed at the self-regard which had not left him despite his new attire.

Yet even as he thought of touching Narayan's feet in reverence, Narayan surprised him by making a pointless remark, speaking purely as a lawyer.

'You know, it wasn't necessary to give up the gold. You could have maintained that the account was a forgery, and not in Tripathi's handwriting. If the son had gone to court over it, he would certainly have lost the case.'

*

Dinakar felt relieved by Narayan's worldliness, even though just a moment ago Narayan's large-hearted speech had created a dilemma for him. Seeing how a man such as Narayan could overcome his limitations in a noble gesture made Dinakar feel small. If he had responded by touching Narayan's feet, that act would also have increased his own self-esteem, and would not have been a sign of turning over, in facing a truth.

'What was I really feeling as Narayan told of his affair with Gangu?' Dinakar wondered. 'Was it regret? When I pressured her the first time, she had appeared ignorant of such things, yet how soon she began to teach me. Did Gangu, who lost her virginity with me and I with her, then learn from a married man and begin to teach me?'

Dinakar remembered the places and times of meetings with her. Whenever Narayan and his mother went to the temple for darshan, Gangu would quickly pat Gopal to sleep, or leave him to play with one of the children in Tripathi's house, then find some unused corner of the attic where, to the sound of Tripathi reciting mantras, they would join together in love.

'When I was not there, would she meet Narayan in the same place? And when the bedding was spread and the others lay down to sleep, she would sometimes say that she wanted to wander on the bank of the river. Even in that cold we would open the doors of the old temple that Tripathi's ancestors had built and lie together under that stone wall with the big carving of Ganesh on it. On the stone floor that was damp with oil, sandal-paste, and kumkum. And again we would lie together in Kashi, where I went with them because she asked me to go. In my very small room. On a torn mat.

'Where could she have met Narayan when everyone was sleeping side by side? Could he even have had her when his mother was sleeping in the same room? I had thought that all Gangu's stolen moments were mine alone. Where else, when she was out of my sight, could she have been meeting him? At Hardwar? At Kashi? At Mathura?

'I used to get up early every morning to bring buckets of hot water to people staying in the dharamshala, to the very old and the very young who couldn't go in the cold to bathe in the Ganga. And then in the afternoon I had to serve food to everyone. I had taken these duties on myself during my holidays . . . perhaps that was when Narayan had his stolen moments with her.

'Or could it have been when I visited the houses of my classmates?' He remembered that Gangu used to tell him, 'You may become bored being with me always. Take some time for yourself, go and wander about and then come back. I will be waiting.'

'Perhaps when Gangu became pregnant and confessed to Narayan about her affair with me, he suffered in the same way I am suffering now,' Dinakar thought. 'Like me, he must have searched his memory, wondering when she made love with me without him ever knowing. If he dwells on the details of my lovemaking and I think of the details of his lovemaking, how can he or I ever cross over and realize the illusion of samsara? On the contrary, we keep on lusting feverishly. Searching, questioning, we chew the same stuff and regurgitate like a cow that chews its cud, swallowing it over and over again. Until we love another woman, we keep wandering like wraiths.'

Even as he thought this, Dinakar became aroused and again desired Gangu, wanting her even if it meant deceiving his friend. He thought of her years ago, gasping, getting him into her urgently, in the secretive darkness. When he had seen her come down the stairs just now, her middle-aged beauty had stirred him, got him vibrating with pleasure. She had been his first lover, she had made the pleasure of woman bloom for him and had remained in him like a fragrance. Thinking of this, he sighed, feeling sure that for him there would be no liberation from bhava. The sigh was not of sorrow, but of weariness. Of desire which had begun to wither.

Narayan, released from his lawyerly self, began to speak again. And again Dinakar listened and suffered, as if he were dreaming in the cool moonlight on the clean white sands of the beach.

16

'Gangu's son is named Prasad. Since we didn't know whose son he was, we called him the prasad of Hardwar.'

Narayan spoke half jokingly, reaching out to include Dinakar. There was in him a touch of urbane courtesy, as if—even after twenty-five years—he were asking, 'Do you approve of the name?' Dinakar respected Narayan for this, and felt that his friend had gone beyond him. But what Narayan went on to say pushed him into a sorrow that would remain with him.

'Until Prasad was five years old, Gangu and I would meet in her house secretly, without any anxiety. Chandrappa was our protector. When she and I were together, he would be breaking logs outside the gate, or drawing water from the well for the flower garden. If anyone came and asked for her, he would say, "Gangu not there." It used to pain me that this dull-wit could comprehend so much. I do not know what Gangu felt about it. How could we ever repay Chandrappa?

'As Prasad grew, so did our anxieties. Our lovemaking became a matter of haste. It seemed to me that she always wanted it to be over quickly. And since she was eager for it to be over as soon as possible, my attention got distracted. I also thought of you. How, after taking your pleasure, there was no need for you to have anything more to do with Gangu. You had become invisible for us. But because of Prasad, you stayed in my mind.

'As Prasad grew older, he became unhappy because the other children at school made fun of him. My son Gopal also seemed discontent. Although he had grown up under Gangu's care, if she came to see him, he would get irritable. He became quiet only if my mother rebuked him. And it made me uneasy, thinking that I was leading an immoral life using my mother's protection. But such guilt leads nowhere. We don't get liberated from maya by such feelings. Anyhow, as I became well known, everyone accepted me. My relations with Gangu became a secret that everyone knew.

'Yet I stopped going to meet her when Prasad was at home. Gradually, it became more and more difficult to make love discreetly. This has been so for the past ten years. It is far more than ten years now since we have been able to meet without strain, because one day Prasad openly said to his mother, "Let him marry you if he is my father." Somehow I could not take that step, and I suffered because of it. But what is the use of such suffering?

'Prasad stopped going to school. He would sit moodily in the house. Gangu had done well as a teacher, but she too began to suffer, keeping her son's unhappiness in her belly. Yet nothing changes if we groan, we just keep on groaning. And how could she ever leave me?

'Then everything changed when Prasad started to learn music. He developed and got better. But he wouldn't sing to just anyone, though when he comes to our house, he always sings bhajans for my mother. He wouldn't sing even to his own mother. And if I came anywhere near him, he would stop singing.

'The mystery was that he would sit in his own room and sing for hours before Chandrappa. And Chandrappa, whom we thought a dumb animal, would listen for hours, sitting in front of Prasad with his mouth hanging open. Before and after singing, Prasad would bow to Chandrappa and to his tamboura.

'But all along Prasad must have been developing vairagya. He even began to seem tolerant of me. If he smiled at me I would be happy the whole day, forgetting all the irritations that Gopal caused me. Prasad looked exactly like the holy sage Shuka, as my mother also said. His serene eyes, long beard, hair falling onto his shoulders, the white clothes—dhoti and dhotra—in these he looked just like a young sage. I would think, "He is nobody's son, he is God's son," and feel at peace.

'But this morning something happened. Prasad went and stood before his mother and asked, "Who am I?"

'Gangu said that her eyes filled with tears because she couldn't lie to this son of hers who looked like a rishi, yet she did not want to speak the truth. She also felt confused, and wondered why Prasad should now be asking this, when for so long he had been made fun of as my son. But then she understood that Prasad wasn't asking her that question, he was questioning himself. And having asked, "Who am I?", he added, "Mother, I want to take sanyas to understand this question. I want to go to Hardwar where my life took root, and there I will also meditate on the roots of music. Please give your permission for this. The attachments of samsara are difficult to break. So I will also take Appayya with me. He seems very devoted to me." As you know, it is only

Chandrappa whom Prasad calls "Appayya". After saying all this, he touched his mother's feet.

'Gangu now feels desolate and deeply troubled because of what Prasad said this morning. She does not know what will become of her if she loses her only son.

'She spoke to me of ways to keep her son. Should we tell him the truth of his birth? That would mean telling about you too. So you see, your coming just now must have been fated. Gangu has the illusion that her son will stay back in her house once he learns the whole truth. Another illusion is that if she gets a wedding thread tied by me before God, her son's agitation will end.

'I do not see what relationship there is between the two. Perhaps to my lawyer's mind things don't happen that way. Still, I agreed to tie the thread. But now I am worried about Gopal. Maybe my greedy son will even want to kill me, fearing that the property will be divided. Haven't I already seen what his politics is like? He gets his opponents beaten by thugs.'

Narayan once again started sounding like a lawyer.

'Since Prasad is a vairagi, I will have all my property registered in my son's name, even that which is not ancestral property, but out of my own earnings. I have already registered Gangu's property in her name. Anyhow, what she earns is enough for her. But I am still worried about my mother. I know that she will accept my tying the marriage-thread on Gangu. One day she saw me looking worried, and said to me meaningfully, "Find a girl for your son and get him married. He can live separately with his family. He will learn to be responsible. Then you can do what you please." After saying this, she surprised me even more by what she said next in a whisper.'

Narayan stopped talking, opened the door of the car, waited for Dinakar to be seated, and then started the engine.

'Do you know what Mother told me?' Narayan asked, beginning to drive the car.

He paused, and then continued in a respectful tone, 'For my mother there will be no need to take another birth. Although she lives in this bhava, she is free from it.'

After some time he spoke again, his voice trembling.

'What Mother whispered to me was, "Gangu is like a member of our family." She said this to me a year ago. I told Gangu and she said, "Because of Amma's words, I have truly become your wife." '

Dinakar felt depleted. He thought, 'I am part of Narayan's life, but have no role to play in his release. He is framed by the samsara of his daily world, and I don't have that. There are people to advise him, people to listen to him, society to look

out for. He has a place in society, but I don't.
There are people to whom he can cause pain,
people who expect things from him, but I have
none. Prasad exists for Narayan, not for me. Prasad
may be my son, or he may not be, but there is
nothing for me to do about it. It is as if I am
dangling, not knowing in which direction I should
turn. And this body cannot endure being
directionless indefinitely. For a rudderless man
like me, there is neither samsara nor sanyas. I can't
be in the world or be out of it. I have no ground
to stand on. No matter how much I search, I will
never find who I am.'

17

Narayan Tantri turned his car off the main road. He was still speaking, but Dinakar couldn't hear what he said. Stopping in front of an isolated tile house, Narayan surprised Dinakar by saying, 'I come here sometimes when I want a drink.' Dinakar began to feel suspicious when Narayan entered the house as if it were his own, and a fellow sitting outside, with only a towel over his bare shoulder, stood up and shouted, 'Rangamma, lawyer has come!' Dinakar thought, 'Ah, this Narayan is also like me. He cannot keep up a strong emotion for a long time.' A dark attractive woman showed her face and, while chewing paan, said to Narayan in welcome, 'Have you come? And after so many days . . .'

Narayan didn't have to say anything more. She brought a jug of water and a bottle of whisky and placed them before him. 'I have given up drinking for as long as I wear these clothes,' said Dinakar. But he felt tempted, remembering his Delhi days as he smelt the whisky Narayan poured out. While Dinakar was admitting to himself that he would very soon return to his drinking, Narayan told Rangamma in Tulu, 'This is my friend from Delhi, a very great man. He is now in vrata. Bring him some lemon sherbet. No other requirements today.'

Rangamma went inside flirtatiously. Dinakar thought, 'So this too is part of Narayan's condition. He suffers, yet keeps his consolations intact. And when he thinks, "There is no use in mere suffering," he becomes a vedantin. But like me, he will not turn over and be made new.'

Dinakar felt ashamed of the way he was thinking. Here was Narayan, truly suffering, boldly getting ready. to marry Gangu. 'Why should I judge him because of Rangamma when I myself have never been innocent? There is no liberation without clarity. And there is no clarity for me as long as I live in this world.

'Once Ramakrishna Paramahansa put food before Kali and said, "Mother, you must eat this." When she didn't eat it he began to cry, and then a black cat came and ate the food. Ramakrishna believed that the black cat was Kali herself.

'If I were there, I would think it was just a cat, not a goddess. I can't even regret that I would believe so. Anyhow, it truly was a black cat. I am sure that if it had seen a mouse, it would have eaten it.

'For people like me and Narayan, there is no clarity and there are no miracles, no wonderment, no turning over. There is no satisfaction in samsara either. Nor can I be content with not wanting to know what is beyond the world, even while I live in the world. Which means I have neither heaven nor hell, I have only small daily miseries.'

Narayan, who had been enjoying his whisky, suddenly became expansive.

'I think that the only vice I have hidden from my mother is my drinking. But maybe Mother pretends not to know in order that I should keep thinking she doesn't know. What use is there in worrying about what we have become? We should just keep quiet. God's grace will come to those who keep quiet.

'Never mind that. Think of Shastri who brought you here. Do you know that he had a wife like gold and he beat her so much that she ran off with a Malayali pundit? She took with her a trunk full of gold. But Shastri also has a keep. She was there from the beginning. She is a very nice woman. On her advice, he married a second time. He had a daughter who became disgusted with his ill temper and ran away with someone. Now Shastri goes around with Purana and pravacchan, thinking he can lose his karma like this, talking and talking. Mad brahmin! There is a proverb that the nature you are born with will not leave you even if you are burnt to ashes. Even if people change, others won't believe it. All over this province they say that Shastri killed his wife and that the jackfruit tree which he planted in the pit where he buried her has never borne a single fruit. And some people say he has hidden his own gold.'

Intoxicated by his own words, Narayan began to praise Gangu.

'I used to take my drinks in Gangu's house. I would write on a piece of paper, and poor Chandrappa would take it and bring whisky and ice from a shop. Later I had a fridge put in Gangu's house. My mother had said, "There can be no fridge in our house." She believes in madi. You see? Gangu's son probably did not like my drinking whisky in their house. Gangu held my feet and begged, "Don't drink here, please." But when I stopped drinking there, I also stopped going there. I developed a new habit of coming here. This is what we mean by samsara.

'But I haven't asked you anything about yourself. Also, Gangu asked me about you. You know what answer I gave her? "Artists like him don't get married, they live a carefree life," I told her. And do you know what Gangu said? She said, "He looks as if he is in some deep sorrow."

Narayan began to laugh. All the pain in his mind seemed to have disappeared.

18

Shastri had returned and was waiting. Narayan
went upstairs to his bedroom, on the pretext that
he didn't want dinner, because he didn't want his
mother to catch the smell of whisky. But Sitamma
anyway mixed some beaten rice with curd and
sent it to his room. She could not send cooked
food because hands and eating-place could not be
washed after the meal. When Shastri mentioned
that he didn't take cooked food at night, she
served beaten rice and curd to him too. For Dinakar
and her grandson Gopal, she served a grand dinner.

This was very different from the afternoon
meal. All around a cured banana leaf were different

vegetable side-dishes, and also lentil salad, poppadom—crispy fried poppadom—kheer, a little dal—all of these things were like an artistically designed menu-card. Some items which were not visible now would appear later on.

To please Sitamma, Dinakar—like her grandson Gopal—took some water in his cupped palm, dripped a little through his fingers around the edge of the leaf, and drank the rest before starting the meal. Sitamma asked, 'Do brahmins in your part follow this ritual?' Dinakar didn't understand her and looked at Gopal, who explained. Dinakar nodded 'Yes' to Sitamma, then turned and told Shastri, 'It is from this second mother that I came to know of kuttavalakki. If my mother was from this side, she must also have fed me that.'

Then he asked Sitamma for some kuttavalakki and she said, 'Don't fill your belly with this. That's stuff that only old people eat when they are fasting in the evening.'

Once again, just as he had at their first meeting, Shastri stared at Dinakar while he ate kuttavalakki. He was startled when Sitamma laughed and said, 'Why do you stare at that boy as if you want to eat him up?'

Shastri prayed to himself, 'O Bhagavati, protect me. When I look at him, I see in his face the radiance of Pundit. His eyes are like his mother's, but his short nose, his complexion, the firmness

with which his lips press together, all these are
like Pundit's. When Pundit listened to music, he
used to sit in just that way. He must be Pundit's.'

Then he thought, 'No, he must be my child. I
begot him while I was in that mad howling. Yet
through some maya, he received a tender nature.
He is mine, but he is not like me. He's a perpetuator
of my family. Yet I cannot claim him.' He began to
sob inwardly, thinking, 'My doubts will never be
cleared. It will be my karma to go to hell and be
wailing there alone for eternity. O Bhagavati, show
this old man the path. Burn away my hatred for
Pundit. Release me.'

Having made this prayer, Shastri finished his
tiny meal. He spent the whole night thinking
about meeting Dinakar the next day, asking
himself, 'Should I take him to my house, where
the ghost is? Or should I not take him?' Because of
worry over this, he did not sleep.

Next day, when Dinakar got up, he said to
Shastri, 'When I come back from Kerala I will
come and stay with you, all right, Uncle?'

'Why should Dinakar say this?' Shastri thought,
feeling cheered by Dinakar's words. 'It must be
the Devi's wish that I have to wait before deserving
to take my son home.' With this in his mind, he
left, after breakfast, in his car.

Being old, not having much longer to live,
Shastri thought that he had lost his desire for life.

He went to Radha's house feeling relieved by that thought. 'When I die, who will perform my funeral rites?' he had once asked himself. But now he was content to leave it to God, and told himself, 'Let whatever is true be revealed.'

19

When Dinakar went to his room that night, he couldn't sleep. He got up and squatted on his bed, tried to listen to music on his Walkman, but now the Tibetan chanting seemed unreal. There was no response to it in his heart.

Dinakar decided to write letters. His first letter would be to someone who, with him as catalyst, had become a holy woman. He would write for his own sake, because he knew she would never read the letter, and his knowing this impressed on him his absurd state.

He began writing in English:

'Dear Shrimati Mahamata,'

He laughed at himself, struck it out, and, more properly, still in English, began again.

'Dear Mahamata,'

—and on top of the page, to please her, he wrote in Devanagari, *om namo bhagavati*.

'Dear Mahamata,

When, in my troubled days, I was trying to understand my relations with you and Gangu, I read a story about you in the *Illustrated Weekly*. The story went something like this:

One night you were travelling to Kashi in a train, and you saw a handsome young man. At that moment, you suddenly recalled that you had been Radha in a previous birth. A divine love welled up in you and you became helpless. Your body, which belongs to this bhava, could not bear this experience. You even forgot that your father was there with you. When the train stopped for a little while in some station, you got off with only the clothes you were wearing and from there you began wandering about like a religious mendicant. Once, while wandering, you felt tired and sat under a bodhi tree. It was then that you saw a cowherd playing on a flute. He, like the handsome young man you had seen on the train, was Bhagavan Shri Krishna himself, come to release you from your cycle of births. Listening to his flute, you were liberated from this world and became Radha herself.

This was, in short, your history as given in the story. There were also some pictures of you as you look now. Yet I could immediately see that the old mischievous look had not disappeared from your eyes.'

'Dear Mahamata,

It is from me, not Krishna, that you had your first great experience of love in this bhava. From looking at me, who these days is in spiritual anguish. Listen, and I will make you remember.

Twenty-four years ago, you must have been eighteen then. By chance I was travelling in the same second-class compartment. You were sleeping on an upper berth, your father was sleeping in the berth below you. As you told me later on, your father had brought you to Kashi to overcome your bad planets because you had refused to live with your husband. You were still a girl studying in college and you told me all this in your beautiful broken English.

But here is the important point. My berth was near yours and I could see that your berth was not properly held by the chain. That was a good excuse for me to watch you anxiously. You had been looking at me, too, your eyes filled only with me. Your father was watching me suspiciously, but you didn't know this. Very gently, you began to bite your lips and move your mouth as if you were chewing something. You pushed up your breasts as if they were a heavy weight, then looked at the fan as if feeling hot. Under cover of your bedsheet, you began opening the buttons of your sari blouse. You smoothed your hair and even winked, showing me you understood that I wanted to bite your lips. Your eyes were very mischievous, eyes that smiled on their own. Even now your eyes are like that.

I had been thinking of my love for a girl called Gangu a year before, a love that had dissolved our bodies. Now I was looking at you, wanting to eat you up, yet trying to behave as if the only reason I looked at you was my concern that, without being properly secured, your berth might fall. I came over and, making as if to fix the chain, brought my left arm near your thighs. Then you turned slightly and with your right thigh touched my left arm.

While I was lifting the berth slightly so that I could attach the hook, your father got up, started hitting me, and shrieked, "Hey! Ay, ay!" Fortunately, other passengers in the compartment appreciated my concern, appreciated that a young man dressed in modern clothes responded so courteously to a woman in distress. They scolded your father, who had an irritable expression on his face. You still watched all this mischievously, and had silently come to an understanding with me.

I have always been good at knowing the heart of a woman, even in the clothes I wear right now. I acted as if I had been insulted by your hot-headed father, yet had forgiven him. After everyone switched off their lights, you quietly got down from your berth and made your way along the aisle. I guessed where you had gone and, a little later, I followed and pushed open the toilet door. You were waiting inside, and you embraced me. Not only had you opened the buttons of your blouse, you had even removed your brassiere and tucked it into the waist of your sari.

The stench of urine didn't bother us. I began biting your lips. You kissed me all over my face and ears, took my hands to your breasts. You murmured that you were a college student and hated the marriage that had been forced on you. You would go with me anywhere I wanted. In your reckless intensity of passion you seemed like a goddess to me. The train slowed, to stop at a station. Then you said, "Let's get down here and run away."

Although I felt great desire for you, I had no courage. Yet I said, "Yes, yes," as if saying so were a part of foreplay, and began to touch you everywhere.

But you were a wild girl. You left the toilet and got down from the train. It moved off again almost immediately. Soon your father noticed your absence. He shouted and searched for you, then gathered together all the bundles of luggage and got down at the next station.

After Gangu, you were my second withdrawal. Both times I withdrew, and this made me doubtful of myself. I thought I might be incapable of real love, that I was perhaps obsessed only with my own self.

Years passed, and I became famous. After

many love affairs, I finally married. When I found that my wife was happier in someone else's bed than in mine, I felt furious and humiliated. I was disgusted by our quarrels over how much gold I should give her in order to divorce me. Despite my disgust, I didn't turn over. I didn't change. Just as she had married me for my wealth and kept up another relationship, I—in my own glamorous world—was balancing a few other relationships, like a tightrope walker in a circus. You may say that since I did not experience the truth of who I am, I suffered the illusion of being held captive by this bhava. Although I had known this truth intellectually, it was delectable to be under the spell of such intrigues. Forgetting the time I promised to one woman, I promised the same time to another; cheating on one in order to placate another; using the anger and emotion that I caused as a spice to make the act of love more delicious—this became an addiction. Yet it also led to a certain weariness that made it possible for me to listen, however dimly, for another strain of melody in me.

I wasn't able to live with my wife. Yet, for the sake of convention, I felt unable to leave her. Then one day I was drinking fine Darjeeling tea with her in the Taj Intercontinental, and I simply got up and left, went to the bank, and brought back some of the gold which my mother had left for me. I placed before her bars of gold worth nearly twenty lakhs of rupees, and she was wonderstruck. I will never forget the way her face bloomed. I saw in her the delight of an innocent child, and felt touched by the play of illusion that the gold produced in her. It seemed then that my hatred for her disappeared.

But that hatred returns whenever I remember the sounds of her lovemaking with the other man. One evening, I had entered the flat with my own key and stood silently in the drawing room. I heard her moaning in ecstasy. Her lover was a mere dull engineer. They were like two animals making strange sounds and then getting spent. I couldn't bear it, and thought of taking a knife from the kitchen and slashing her. Even the most lustful man will find it astonishing that his woman would get done to her by another person what he himself does. Why shouldn't there be release even in such painful astonishment?

Anyhow, seeing her enthralled by the illusion of gold, I thought I had a glimpse of my possible release. I took this Ayyappa vrata, postponed all other engagements, and for three months wandered in holy places. But I found no peace of mind. Then I read the story about you. That gave me hope of another way of release, and about a week ago I came to your world-famous ashram near Madras.

Such crowds of people, such jubilance! Everywhere there were colour pictures of you, clothes with your picture, stickers with your picture, plates with your picture. From the outside your ashram looked like a modern shopping place. I felt a little disappointed, but also curious. There were dharamshalas with rooms where people could stay in whatever degree of luxury they could afford. But I stayed in a resort hotel which had been built in a village on the beach, where quite a few foreign devotees also stayed.

Even if you personally met everyone for a minute, and sat like a Bhagavati Devi for ten hours, you could still see only six hundred people a day. Although I hid my identity as a TV man from everyone else, I revealed it to your managers, and so after three days I was lucky enough to get your darshan. There was a queue about a kilometre long, where each person got a half-minute with you. I had been standing in another, smaller queue. This was for VIPs who would get a full minute with you. There I had to wait, hopeful and uncertain, for darshan of your face—I who was an agent of that great change in you.

The half-minute queue people were fortunate enough to have their heads touched by your hand; but those in the one-minute queue were fortunate enough to be embraced by you. I had heard one of the mysterious tales that the pilgrims told each other: whoever has pure bhakti, whoever is standing on tiptoe, poised for release, having worn away all the karma and dirt of this becoming—when you embraced such people, it was said, your breasts would leak milk. If milk appeared, you would press it to that person's eyes. There was an old judge of the Supreme Court who got your milk, then gave up everything and stayed on to help manage your ashram.

Waiting anxiously for my turn, getting nearer and nearer, I counted on my watch the good fortune of the people standing in front of me—I wanted at least to glimpse you when I moved up in the queue. But your officers had arranged the queue in such a zigzag maze that no one could catch sight of you until they were almost face-to-face. Perhaps the intent was to make you suddenly appear like a vision.

But gradually I lost interest in following the process. Because of my TV shows, I too am adept at timing. And hadn't I come in search of you because I was tired of such games? Just like those who become artists in sexual matters and who deliberately stage the climax of an erotic experience.

Then I saw you. It surprised me that you did not seem tired, even after touching so many people. You embraced me, but I was not a blessed one who brought milk to your breasts. Did I or didn't I see the old mischievousness in your eyes? Have you or haven't you truly crossed over? But even after turning over, don't we still remain limited by our bhava? You still urinate, don't you? You embraced me just as I was thinking all these things.

You enfolded me in a divine, never-stale-however-much-touched love. I was filled with a sense of wonder. Then you went on and embraced the person standing next to me. But when you had embraced me, you made me feel for that moment that only I existed for you, just as you made the next person feel that you existed only for him. I thought that this might be a gift which never tires you although you do it day after day after day. I also felt sad that you, always sitting there that way, had grown fat despite your young age.

After having your darshan, I took up my journey again to seek out an old woman named Sitamma, who years before had become like my mother, and also to look for Gangubai, who had secretly shown me the taste of this body which I am now trying to punish in my vairagya. During this journey I also met an old man called Shastri. He fed me kuttavalakki and became like a relation from some past life.

My dear Mahamata, is the son of Gangu, whom both Narayan and I had loved, my son? It seems he intends to sacrifice all attachments in vairagya. Tell me, what should I do now?'

In this way, Dinakar finished the letter, felt tired, and slept.

20

On his third day at Sitamma's house, Dinakar thought that he had woken up very early, but when he came out he found that Sitamma had woken up earlier still, had already swept and sprinkled the veranda, and was ready to lay the rangoli. 'Did you sleep?' she asked. 'Bring a chair and sit down. Look what rangoli I am going to lay. I will fill the whole veranda with the picture of Sri Chakra which is on your amulet. Isn't that rakshe from your mother?' And she began to work.

'Sri Chakra' were the only words he had understood. But as he watched, he grasped little by little what began to rise on the veranda in red kumkum and yellow turmeric, and when it had fully arisen he took in the whole thing again, all the while drinking fresh coffee.

Nine triangles joining, one inside the other, creating an orbit which becomes a circle in turn becoming a chakra, the chakra becoming a petalled flower, the flower a form manifested within a square opened out to the four directions, the whole figure wombing in itself the creative energy of earth and sky.

This form had perfected itself in Sitamma's meditation, so that the eyes of an observer became absorbed in the continuous intermingling of yoni and linga, resting in the colours of kumkum and turmeric, then moving towards the point at the centre, becoming one with it.

After his coffee Dinakar felt serene, went upstairs to his room and again sat down to write, this time to the wife from whom he had separated.

*

'Dear Ranjana,

In the extreme hatred and jealousy I felt that day, I see now a hint of my release. I had wanted to take a knife from the kitchen and kill you. But even for a slut like you, there might have been a possibility of release in getting fucked by him. I have begun to believe this now that I can, without any jealousy, imagine that moment when you opened out continuously to him, allowing him to enter into every nook and corner of yourself, as you moaned in ecstasy. It is possible to get free of bondage through an unearthly pleasure so intense that you feel you cannot bear it, that you will die.

But if you continue to be a scheming slut all your life, you will never completely turn over. I am writing this after seeing that a girl who was touched by me in her ecstasy of passion became a mahamata. There was also a hint that vairagya might flower in you when I saw your face bloom in the ecstasy of illusion while looking at the gold I gave you. I cannot guess where you might find release. But if it happens, you will realize how easy it always was, how it could have happened at any time, how at any time you could have turned over as easily as turning over in your sleep. I wish you success in this. I never truly touched you and reached you. You have never truly touched me and held me. I hope that someday I will find it amusing that I still sometimes feel jealous when I think of another man caressing the birthmark on

your thigh. Why do you want to get fucked
by a worthless scum like him? I can't
understand why you want to get fucked by
a man who enjoys leftovers. Keep my flat as
long as you want. Don't worry that I may
suddenly turn up there. I am sending by
registered post my key to the flat, so that I
am not even tempted to do so. One thing
more. Whatever I bought during the year of
our marriage because you desired it, is
yours.

From one feeling weary because of you, still
not free from hatred, searching for a way
out—

Dinakar'

Then he thought of all his other lovers and
began writing short notes to them.

'Dear Sudarshini,

I never loved you wholeheartedly. You too
did not fully love me. But we were eager to
conquer each other.

I remember seeing you one day, humming
to yourself, sitting alone and looking
inwards. In such moments I see the
possibility that you may be released from
bhava.

Dinakar'

'Dear Priti,

Your desire for me grew from the fear that your youth was fading. And I, always curious in the beginning about every woman, came together with you. But later I began to search for ways to escape from you. Yet I held you to me through some illusion of love. That's because, like you, I am lonely.

Now I believe that you pretended to enjoy sex with me even when you didn't, because you wanted to cheat yourself. Forgive me for pretending to believe that you were happy. I remember one day you carefully removed the jasmine from your braid and placed the flowers on a green leaf. With your fingers, you delicately sprinkled water, the right amount, with loving tenderness. You were not aware that I, in wonderment, was watching you do this. Remembering this now brings hope that some good will come to us from that moment.

Desiring desirelessness, and realizing that it can't be got by desiring it,

Yours,
Dinakar'

'Dear Mamata,

You never allowed me to see you naked.

But one day as you quickly removed your clothes to get under the blanket, I saw a white patch on your thigh. I knew that it was not leprosy, but you feared I might think so. Your liberation might lie in the leucoderma itself, even if it spreads all over your body. May God give you strength to face it.

You made many sacrifices for me. You accepted all my other lovers without envy.

I was never truly excited by you. It was feelings of compassion that united us.

Praying for you,

Dinakar'

He put all the letters that he had written into envelopes, thinking that he would write still more letters the next day—to one in Lucknow, to another in Allahabad, to another in Kuwait, to yet another whom he had been trying to seduce and who had been putting him off to make the desire more delicious—a reporter for a Delhi paper. Perhaps there was no use in sending the letter to Mahamata, who hardly had time to breathe. He stepped out of the house to go in search of a mailbox.

Sitamma called to him and said, 'As soon as you finish walking, take a bath and eat your food. I'm going to make dosa for you today. I don't know what time my great son will get up. He has court today.' He found the affection and concern in her voice very pleasant.

21

Narayan, on his way to take a bath, came to Dinakar's room and closed the door. Then he said, 'I do not know what to do.'

The previous night Narayan had come in drunk, awakened his son, and told him of his resolve to marry Gangu. He had reassured Gopal that he would sign over all his property to him. 'But my great son danced about in fury, shouting, "Why should I have been a son to such a father?"'

Gopal had also abused Gangu, who had brought him up, calling her an avaricious prostitute, and he cursed Prasad as a hypocritical sanyasi. Then he beat his head against the wall and screamed,

'How can I stay in such a house?' Nothing of this tantrum was heard in Dinakar's small room upstairs.

But Sitamma had heard the outburst. She had gone to her grandson, consoled him, and told her son Narayan, 'First get this boy married. He may be worried that no one will give him a daughter in marriage. Let his election madness also be over. Whatever he is, isn't he your son? Like his father, this little one wants to become a municipal president and strut about.'

Dinakar was surprised that, in the early morning, Sitamma had been sitting as if unaware of the previous night's outburst. He said to Narayan, 'Your mother is truly a mahamata. She stays in this world, caring for everyone, yet without being entangled with anyone.'

Now, on a flat iron griddle big enough to make four dosas, Sitamma was shaping batter, adding a little ghee, turning the dosas over to make them crisp, and when they were nearly ready, applying a little red chutney, filling them with potato and onion mixture, folding them, then lifting them off neatly and placing them directly on the leaf-plate. More green chilli chutney was served on the side. So her cooking too was devoted to God, and in the perfection of her dosas Dinakar saw the same dexterity of hand which had made the nine triangles meet in sacred unity.

Hoping that, if he spoke English, his mother would not recognize his distress, Narayan said to Dinakar, 'My son Gopal, who I am certain was born to me and who has legitimate status, I do not feel is my son at all.'

Having said this, Narayan changed the topic out of a kind of delicacy, sensing that what he would otherwise go on to say might embarrass his friend. He turned the question into one of having a common personal law for the whole country, and waited for Dinakar's opinion. Having already eaten two masala dosas at Sitamma's urging, Dinakar—after more urging—began to eat a crispy plain dosa. Then Chandrappa's voice was heard calling 'Amma!' Sitamma, who was about to serve a dosa to her son, brought it instead to the backyard on a banana leaf. After serving it to Chandrappa, she came in.

'Chandrappa asked whether Gangu should come here to see lawyer or go to his office in the city,' she said. 'I told him, "Let her come here at least for a moment, even if she has not taken a bath. Then she could also have hot dosa. Isn't it a holiday for her today, and doesn't she always make gruel for everyone in her house?" Since it would anyhow take time to make gruel, I asked her to come here. She can also bring dosas for all of them. Anyway,' she continued to Narayan, 'what is your big hurry? The office is always there, you can reach half an hour later. I don't know why my royal grandson hasn't come for his food yet. The little one is always at the phone and forgets to eat.'

So, speaking in her sprightly manner, she went inside to see if there was enough batter for Gangu's dosas and, seeing that there was enough and more, she lowered the stove's flame and asked Narayan, 'Shall I give you another?' Gratified when he belched in satisfaction, she went to the backyard to speak to Chandrappa. But Chandrappa had already left, having thrown the used leaf-plate into the bin outside.

outside.

22

Gangu, in another of her beautiful saris with
matching glass bangles, and wearing jasmine in
her long braided hair, looked fresh from her bath.
Sitamma served her dosas in a separate dining
room kept for Narayan's friends who were not
orthodox. After finishing the dosas, Gangu threw
the leaf outside, and although she had been told it
was unnecessary to purify the eating-place with
cow-dung and water, Gangu nonetheless cleansed
the place where she had sat and eaten, and then
went upstairs to meet Narayan.

When their conversation was finished,
Narayan—dressed in a black coat, white pants, a

bow-tie under his starched white collar, and with a gown and some files in his hand—came downstairs with Gangu, who was behind him. She touched Dinakar's feet and asked in Hindi, 'Will you come in the evening? Your Prasad said that he wanted to meet you.'

Noting with admiration the Hindi she had learnt in school, Dinakar agreed to come. Narayan said, 'Gangu's house is close by. Just walk on the road opposite to our house for a while, then turn to your right, and soon you will come to a mailbox. From there, turn to your left and go a little distance, until you see the Syndicate Bank. If you stand in front of the bank, you will see a narrow pathway to the left. Hers is the fifth house on the path. It is named "Rishikesh." A fitting house for Prasad,' Narayan said, laughing.

Dinakar suddenly remembered their visit to Sivananda's Ashram in Rishikesh. One day Narayan, carrying a howling Gopal, went with Sitamma back across the bridge, and Dinakar and Gangu had unexpectedly enjoyed a rare moment of privacy. And this was the same Gangu who now stood before him expressionlessly.

Then Narayan said, 'Never mind, Gangu, better to send Chandrappa along with Dinakar, let him not lose his way,' and turning to Dinakar, he added, 'Come with me now to the office, I must speak to you. I will send you back later in the car.'

He took Dinakar's arm and led him to the car.
Gangu stayed back to share her news with
Sitamma.

While driving, Narayan talked to Dinakar as if
he had just been saved from a big crisis. Gangu
had told him how afraid she had been that morning
when she saw Prasad with his head shaved. But
after finishing his musical practice, Prasad touched
her feet, stood up before her and said, 'Let Narayan
Tantri start coming home. I will also live at home,
although I will go away sometimes and stay at
other places.' He also told her that he didn't want
the attachment even of saffron robes.

'Do you understand, Dinakar? This was the
first time he ever spoke my name to Gangu. She
could hardly believe it. And Prasad spoke of me
with affection and calm. He has shed his hatred of
me. Gangu told me all this with tears in her eyes.
When the son becomes a great ascetic like
Adishankara, stands before his mother looking
like a bestower of fearlessness, would not his
mother feel as if she had been given a new birth?

'Gangu told me, "You don't have to tie a
mangalsutra around my neck for the sake of
appearances." She also told me that, feeling it was
an auspicious moment, she revealed to Prasad the
truth about you. That is why Gangu said that you
should go and bless him. That's why she called
you home. Gangu is a great woman.'

Dinakar felt awkward, hearing Narayan speak with such intensity. Yet in Narayan's words and gestures there was now the ease of one who had been relieved of a great embarrassment. 'I wouldn't be able to achieve the nobility or poise or tactfulness of a man like Narayan who faces crises living in samsara. A man like me is not the man to be morally righteous.' Feeling humbled, Dinakar followed Narayan into his office.

Narayan showed his grand office to Dinakar with pride. There were many clerks, large books, and files. Dinakar admired everything, shook Narayan's hand and, driven by one of Narayan's clerks, came back home.

'Are you not well?' asked Sitamma. She mimed eating, and showed him that she was preparing kesu leaf for lunch.

BOOK THREE

BOOK THREE

23

Radha was weaving a garland of jasmine with banana fibre. Shastri, watching her, said, 'Saroja used to get completely absorbed when she wove jasmine flowers. When she sang, she looked like a Devi.' Then, pacing around the veranda, he added, 'I wish Mahadevi could see her daughter again.' Radha stopped weaving the jasmine and silently prayed, 'Bhagavan, let the moment that I have been waiting for be now.'

It was morning. The young sun rode over clouds, and its early rays shot through now and then. The air was pleasant, and the tidied veranda clean and cool.

Shastri walked about the veranda twice more and said, 'Radha?' He stood silently for a while, clasping his hands behind his back. 'Is he my son? And even if he is my son, would he accept me as his father? He looks like one who may be searching for his father in God. I can only pray that he should succeed. Whether he is my son or not, he seems to be one who can give me a new life. I wish, by God's grace, that the howling within me would stop.'

*

Shastri's blossoming continued as Radha, weeping, revealed the secret that she had been hiding within her.

24

Being a rich landlord, Shastri had placed his daughter in Mangalore College for study. Mangala was an intelligent girl, and he desired that she should have a good education. Mahadevi, anxious to guard her daughter's virtue, had wanted her to stay with a relation. But Shastri had abruptly dismissed her worry. There wasn't anyone he cared to send his daughter to, therefore he put her in a hostel. As a result of this freedom, she became friendly with a boy who was a very good debater. She herself was a bold girl, good at debates, and in her zeal for debating she developed a passion for politics as well. The boy, born in a poor family of

the Malnad Halepyka caste, was intelligent enough
to have got a scholarship to study engineering. He
was handsome, sported a beard, and dressed
attractively in kurta and pyjama.

He had caught the attention of everyone by
changing his name from Thimmaiah to Charvak. It
was like an addiction for him to attract people's
attention by doing something or the other. He
would always use new, striking words to denounce
landlords and casteism. Radha had no
understanding of such things. She only knew that
Mangala had told her that Charvak had gone even
further than a Communist. Mangala was very
impressed by Charvak's arguments, which also
happened to give support to her dissatisfaction
with her father. When she came home, even though
urged by her mother, she wouldn't bow down to
God. And she would argue that all brahmins were
like leeches. Both Mahadevi and Radha took care
not to repeat her ideas to her father.

The change in Mangala's thinking made her
feel close to Radha. She even insisted on eating in
Radha's house. Radha wasn't happy to encourage
this, but she couldn't refuse her food. Mangala
had also confided in Radha about Charvak. 'We
don't believe in marriage. We will work secretly to
bring about a unity among all people and make
revolution,' she had said. In the beginning, when
Mangala talked like this, Radha didn't believe her.

But finally she became convinced that this mad girl was truly serious. She was not like other Mangalore girls. She had no interest in ornaments or clothes, and would make fun of people who were fashionable. She had even made Radha feel that it was shameful to wear gold bangles.

Mangala always dressed in a white sari and white blouse, and she wouldn't put on either earrings or a necklace.

One day, they were arguing and Mangala said, 'Why do you have anything to do with my murderous father who, everyone says, killed his pregnant wife? People like you should be liberated.' She had said this very harshly. Radha thought Mangala very sharp-tongued, just like her father, and kept quiet. In the house of her benefactor, everyone was dear to Radha.

Both Mangala and Charvak gave up college and ran away. God knows where they stayed and what they did for six months, or what they achieved in their revolutionary endeavour. Finally, Charvak came to Shimoga and took up the job of mechanic in a garage. Mangala wrote a letter to Radha saying that what he earned was not enough even for food. 'Don't let my father know where we are. He might kill my husband because he's a shudra. If it isn't a hardship for you and you would like to, send me some money.

Long live revolution!'

*

Radha began to send at least one thousand rupees every month.

But after a few months, Radha noticed a discordant note in Mangala's letters. She regarded this as the ordinary occasional disharmony between husband and wife. But Mangala didn't see this as a question of 'husband-and-wife quarrel lasts until they eat and lie down together.' Instead, she had seen the quarrels as a complication to be found in the lives of all revolutionary activists. Although such explanations were beyond Radha's understanding, she was pleased by Mangala's readiness to confide such things in her.

'Charvak doesn't come home on time, he has begun to drink, and he quarrels with me, saying that by tagging onto a woman like me and taking to family life, he has lost the opportunity to be part of the revolution. But he doesn't seem to realize the true nature of revolution. Only a woman who has become a householder can truly understand the meaning of revolution.' Radha, who had abundant instinctive cunning in such matters, had replied, 'Become pregnant and win over your husband. Everything will be all right.' Mangala listened to this advice without giving up her revolutionary fervour.

'And now your daughter is seven months

pregnant,' Radha told Shastri. 'If you allow me, I will bring her here. Let her deliver in her own mother's house. I will anyhow be there to help.' She said this apprehensively, although adopting a manner of lightness. 'Just because your son-in-law is not a brahmin, you don't have to keep your daughter at a distance. And the child to be born is innocent. What caste can it have? Am I not also a shudra?,' she teased him.

Shastri said, very gravely, 'Bring her.'

Praying to Bhagavati that, by Radha's grace, his mind should keep its calmness, and hoping that the curse on him was at an end, Shastri added, 'I will get a garage in Udupi for that wretched boy. If my daughter is far away from him and there is no one to control him, he will become a drunkard.'

*

Impatient to tell all this to Mahadevi, and excitedly planning how to arrange the house so that his grandchild could be born there, Shastri suddenly thought, as he neared home, 'If Dinakar isn't my son, the gold in that trunk is mine alone, and therefore should belong to my daughter's child.'

Then, as he entered the house, he found himself praying, 'O Bhagavati, let me not think such unworthy thoughts.'

Later, whenever his mind was troubled by

these old conflicts, he would remember that on
this day he had entered the house praying that
such thoughts should never again come to him.

25

Dinakar, having gone up the Shabarimala hill for Ayyappa darshan and come down again, was not surprised to realize that the whole experience had been like a picnic for him. After coming down the hill he bathed in the river and told himself, ' "That" is not to be won if you seek it wilfully.' The river water was cold, and in brisk high spirits he rubbed his body before putting on the new red-bordered Kerala dhoti and white khadi shirt which he had bought before climbing the hill. As he was putting on these clothes, he thought of the winter evening in Mangalore which had shaken him.

Prasad had been sitting in the lotus posture, fingering the strings of the tamboura resting on his arm. When Dinakar, who did not know who his own father or mother were, saw him for the first time, he was filled with desire to know whether Prasad was his son. Yet the image that slowly, gradually, prevailed was of Prasad's long eyes half closed, as if half asleep, in inward-looking contemplation.

The veranda he sat in was open to the skies, and in its soft evening shadow Prasad appeared like the young son of a sage, his lean, strong-muscled body straight-backed, seated in meditation.

Dinakar stood a small distance away, filling his eyes with him. Prasad must have shaved off his long hair and beard only that morning—the shaved portions looked pale, and it was clear that for a long time they had been hidden from the sun. The rest of his body, which was constantly exposed to the sun and wind, was even-toned, the dark Krishna colour which had intoxicated the gopis.

A white cloth was wound around his waist, another white cloth carelessly flung over his shoulder. Dinakar observed that Prasad's nose was long and straight, slightly curved at the tip, that his chin was firm and his forehead broad. Unquestionably, his ears were not Narayan's. But they were certainly not Dinakar's either. They were like Gangu's, the lobes small and delicate. If he wore earrings, the earrings would be perfectly displayed. His whole face had a beauty that would be irresistible to women.

Thinking this, Dinakar recalled his own erotic life and felt shame at his motive in examining Prasad's face so closely.

Then, moved by Prasad's music, he thought, 'But why should I be ashamed? Adishankara must have looked like Prasad when he wrote the commentary to Brahma Sutra. And, although only a boy sanyasi, hadn't Adishankara described the goddess, head to toe, even better than anyone who possessed sexual experience?'

*

Chandrappa, in undershirt and shorts, put aside his hoe and, disregarding the mud on his hands, listened in open-mouthed wonder to Prasad's singing. Dinakar had come and stood in the shaded front garden which was full of parijata, champak, jasmine and hibiscus. It was Chandrappa's labour that had made the whole place so fragrant.

Gangu saw Dinakar looking lovingly at her son. She brought hot milk in a silver cup and placed it on the edge of the pyol, saying in greeting, 'Have you come?' She invited Dinakar onto the veranda. With her pallu draped over her head and sandal-paste on her forehead, she looked like an auspiciously married woman.

Dinakar didn't know how long he sat on the veranda. Shadows lengthened and it became time for lighting the lamps. Prasad was still sitting, singing to himself, motionless. His alap came in waves, returning again and again to the note from which it had emerged. Look, it is simple. Look, now it gathers into complexity. In the enchantment of its rising and falling, it seemed as if Prasad had touched what he wanted to touch.

*

Dinakar felt that the unseen for which he was searching would be like what Prasad had found already. Stillness in motion. Still, even while moving. Because the motion is without resistance, there is stillness. But the sensation can only be fleeting for people like himself. 'What does it matter if he is my son? Or if he is not?' Dinakar thought. Prasad had touched what he himself had not yet touched. What was only a flash for him, Prasad must have gazed at steadily. His entire peaceful being spoke of it—he showed how a person can live in bhava without giving it much regard.

And so Dinakar looked at Prasad as if he were a guru.

It was a sacred moment. Dinakar felt, 'Whether I am his father, whether I am not, I should touch his feet.' Just then, Prasad—like one who lives in the world yet remains untouched by it—opened his eyes, which seemed to have been dwelling in a dream. Without wondering whether this man before him was his father or not, as if curiosity and anxiety had no hold on him at all, he looked at Dinakar, bringing him totally, with complete attention, into his gaze. Dinakar became captive to Prasad's unshakeable calm, and for that moment at least he was fully open, free of any desire or expectation.

*

Prasad touched the tamboura to his eyes and suddenly stood up. At that moment, Dinakar experienced the welling up of love for a child and he thought, 'How sweet-natured and tall and beautiful this boy is.'

Prasad's eyes, which he had found so attractive, closed slowly. Then, standing with folded hands, Prasad went on to prostrate before him, as if to a god. Dinakar, feeling as if he had turned over, stood in awe, and could not find the words for blessing. Gently he touched Prasad's head, and Prasad came to his feet. Then, holding Prasad's face between his hands, Dinakar bent and smelt the crown of his head.

Gangu, watching from a distance, began to cry. She lit the lamp and said, as if to herself, 'From now, my son is a sanyasi. He cannot touch anyone's feet after this. He has himself become the holy feet.'

Then she wiped her eyes with the end of her sari. Despite her sorrow in giving up all motherly hopes for her son, she did not neglect to treat Dinakar courteously, and saying, 'Go, and come again,' walked with him up to the gate.

Afterword

Was it being lost, or drowning in ecstasy?
                                        —Dinakar, in *Bhava*

Towards the end of *Bhava*, the young Prasad—
who already possesses considerable spiritual
stature—stands before his mother and says, 'Who
am I?'

At first, Gangu thinks her son wants to know
who his father is; then she recognizes that Prasad
is announcing his wish to explore the question at
its deepest levels. But Gangu's initial reaction is
understandable. To ask 'Who am I?' can be a
spiritual practice, a mantra, a device for

distinguishing between self and ego ('I' changes; 'I' accumulates layers: what, then, is the nature of my changing and changeable sense of being? And is there a part that doesn't change?); it is also an evanescent thought, a way of locating oneself in society, a means of identifying oneself to one's self—these and other variations on the theme are played out at the heart of *Bhava*.

*

Bhava is like a mystery story, or series of mysteries both factual and metaphysical. (Most of the questions, however, don't get answered.) What happened on the night of Saroja's 'murder'? Did she survive, and later kill herself, or was her death an accident? Had she been seduced—and impregnated—by Pundit? Whose son is Dinakar? Whose son is Prasad? Such concrete questions plot the tale. Perhaps equally compelling are the enigmas of human nature: how did Gangu, who seems so simple and direct, conduct intense, secret love affairs with two men—themselves close friends—at the same time? What explains Saroja's character? Is Pundit a rogue or a saviour? And, more generally, there is the mystery of extremes of being: on the one hand Sitamma, Chandrappa and Radha, who occupy their lives so placidly and unquestioningly; on the other hand Dinakar and Shastri—troubled, unstable, ambivalent—who torment themselves and hurt others.

The two men at the centre of the tale, Shastri and Dinakar, long for relief from uncertainty and anxiety. Their unsettled state of being is signalled by the fact that, when we first encounter them, both wear costumes extravagantly at odds with their inner lives. Despite the traditional garb of puranik (Shastri) and pilgrim (Dinakar), each is acutely aware of the discrepancy between public perception and inner reality, and so feels something of a hypocrite. Yet costumes can be shed. When ripe, the cocoon bursts; when ripe, a person can be transformed, can 'turn over' (as Dinkar thinks of it) as easily as one turns over in sleep.

Shastri is seventy, a far more conventional type than Dinakar, and limited in his taste for subjectivity and self-analysis. Since the death of Saroja, he has tried to redeem himself in the traditional and public spheres: he earns both merit and respect through his role of puranik, reciting ancient tales of the gods and saints. Yet in private life, he continues to be cruel and unable to control his violent temper, especially with his second wife and his daughter. His soul-searching never amounts to much more than wondering, 'Why am I like this?'

But one day Shastri notices that a younger man in his railway carriage is wearing around his neck a Sri Chakra amulet that looks identical to the

one Saroja used to wear, the one she was wearing
when he killed her forty years before. And,
astonishingly, the man resembles Saroja. This
encounter plunges Shastri into crisis. For more
than half a lifetime, he has lived and relived the
guilt, jealousy, rage, fear, and remorse surrounding
his attack on Saroja, whom he had covered with
earth and left for dead. But if the amulet is Saroja's,
it means she might have survived, that he might
not be a murderer after all, and that the man
wearing the amulet could be Saroja's son (and
therefore Shastri's as well).

The shock of realizing that he may not be who
he thought he was readies Shastri for
transformation and a possible rebirth.

*

In *Samskara*, Anantha Murthy's celebrated early
novel, 'The chaste Acharya commits an illicit act,
and as a result his transformation begins' (A.K.
Ramanujan). In *Bhava*, Shastri discovers that he
did *not* commit an illicit act, and as a result his
transformation begins. So Shastri's experience
might be viewed as a perverse inversion of the
Acharya's rite of passage.

Shastri also lives out the Acharya's nightmares.
Soon after Acharya sleeps with Chandri, the
Acharya's wife dies and he decides to 'go where
the legs take me,' and finds himself besieged by

the crude and unfamiliar temptations of the outside world. He feels, '. . . my person has lost form, has found no new form.' As one who has lost his old world and not yet found another, he dreads 'being transformed from ghost to demon.' But this he means figuratively: is he to be released from being like a disembodied ghost (preta), only to become a demon?

For Shastri, the dreaded transformation seems to be enacted literally. At times, he has felt without substance, like 'a ghost in his own house,' but increasingly he feels possessed by a deeply malevolent force, turned into a demon or other evil form. When he rapes Saroja, he couples with her like a demon; when he accuses her of becoming pregnant by Pundit, the 'demon inside him [began] to wail and laugh grotesquely'; when he carries her body to bury her in the pit, 'he strode like a gloating demon.' Years after the crime, he says, 'it seemed this body into which the demon had entered has never learned anything.'

And so, when he sees the amulet on Dinakar's neck, he wonders whether he is about to be possessed once again.

Dinakar, dressed in the black clothing of an Ayyappa devotee, has been undergoing a crisis of his own. That is why he has tried to lose (or find) himself through taking the Ayyappa vow— 'blacking out' his accustomed dress, his eating and drinking habits, even his name, for the forty days of his pilgrimhood. In daily life, he is a famous television star, a man of the world who has had numerous sexual intrigues with women. But it has all come to seem wilful, stale and jaded.

At the end of his Ayyappa pilgrimage, Dinakar—who has lived nearly all his life as an orphan—has gone in search of Sitamma, the 'other mother' whom he had met more than twenty years earlier. He looks forward to her unconditional affection and an experience of renewal through contact with a simple, peaceful life. At forty-five, he is fully, even cynically, aware that he has been shallow and cruel, and that his present spiritual emptiness mirrors the way in which he has chosen to live. He suffers in part because his mind is alert and discerning; a 'modern' man, he is both blessed and cursed with the yearning for an integrated self to which his highly developed self-consciousness is an obstacle.

Dinakar—egotistical, but with a true, if acquired, sensitivity—is of a type that goes far back in Anantha Murthy's fiction, as does the portrayal of unconflicted characters such as Sitamma, who says with intuitive wisdom, 'The whole country thinks this [Dinakar] has grown into a very intelligent man, but this man doesn't even know who is his mother, who is his father, which is his town, so perhaps he wants to believe that God himself is his mother and father and that is why he wears these kind of clothes and goes wandering here and there.' Perceiving Dinakar as rootless and divided, she teasingly reduces his pilgrim's austerities to the wanderings of a little ghost, a little boy in search of home.

*

'Dinakar, reading from an English translation of *Bardo Thodol*, listening on his Walkman to the chanting of Tibetan lamas, tried to relate his present state of mind to the bardo state described in *The Tibetan Book of the Dead*.'

'Shastri began to pray,' "O God, save me from these tormenting doubts which make me like a ghost in limbo." '

Both Dinakar and Shastri (in common with the Acharya) have been caught in a ghostly transitional limbo, like the 'bardo' or 'between-state' of Tibetan tradition. The 'bardo of becoming' for example, connects death and rebirth. *The Tibetan Book of the Dead* says:

'. . . the Bardo or intermediate state which lasts right up until the moment we take on a new birth . . . the bardos . . . are periods of deep uncertainty . . . the seeds of all our habitual tendencies are activated and reawakened.

'. . . The shifting and precarious nature of the bardo of becoming can also be the source of many opportunities for liberation . . .'

'Bardo' is 'equivalent to the Sanskrit term antarabhava', and 'bhava' itself means rebirth (in the Buddhist 'twelve links,' that is, the cycles of death and rebirth).

'Bhava' is also for Anantha Murthy a shortened form of 'bhavavali,' the Jain cycle of death and rebirth—which, unless escaped, is an endless chain of becomings. Although such cycles are also central to Hindu belief, the orientation in *Bhava* is closer to the somewhat existentialist Jain or Buddhist world-view.

*

Dinakar, typically, uses his intellect in trying to comprehend what is happening to him. He thinks of himself in terms of 'bardo,' in terms of 'bhava,' and the nuances of his confusion are nicely displayed in his letters to women—particularly the long, intense outpouring to Mahamata which forms one of the centres of the novel, and in which we get the most sustained and unguarded view of Dinakar. Mahamata has become a holy woman; she does not even recognize Dinakar when he comes to her ashram for darshan; he expects that she will never even see his letter: so he writes as if to a mother/divinity/guru, or as if to a confessor, with the openness and vulnerability one would expect in such a privileged, protected context. Here (and in the other letters as well) he uses 'bhava' to mean 'worldly existence' and 'becoming' interchangeably—even simultaneously.

Unlike Dinakar, Shastri has no such conceptual framework; he lives the nightmare directly, uncomprehendingly—for him the demons, ghosts, burning red eyes, possession by something evil, have all been real. He is like a spirit in limbo, in a between-life-and-death bardo meant to be a transitional phase, but in which the spirit can 'get stuck,' or emerge reborn as a 'hungry ghost.' Terrors of just this sort seem to haunt Shastri. And for more than one reason. He feels condemned to limbo not only because he committed murder, but because in murdering Saroja he may have murdered his own son, the very one who must perform the funeral rites in order to transform him from ghost (preta) to ancestor (pitr).

For Dinakar and Shastri (as for the Acharya, who is perhaps Anantha Murthy's quintessential man-in-transition) the prospect of an endless state of limbo seems unbearable. Yet it is as if we meet Dinakar and Shastri at the point where we take leave of the Acharya. They are going in different directions, shedding different skins; each, in some way, moving towards what the other must leave behind.

The Acharya began as an idealized type with, in effect, a received identity, an inherited dharma with which he feels fully identified; by the end of *Samskara*, he is becoming a self-conscious individual. He has little choice, given that—as he says of sleeping with Chandri—'That act gouged me out of my past world.' With his new 'awareness that I turned over suddenly, unbidden,' he cannot go back to his old identity; therefore any impending rebirth *must* involve individuation and alienation. Shastri and Dinakar, on the other hand, have been alienated for years. They cannot aspire to the sort of innocence that characterizes Sitamma (or the Acharya in his 'past world'), but they would like to achieve a more balanced state, to incorporate something of the serenity that comes from a secure, unconflicted sense of being. They would like to 'turn over' (Dinakar uses the same word as did the Acharya).

*

Dinakar and Shastri receive solace—and glimpses of a possible source of transformation—through literal or symbolic participation in a kind of life which calms their demons. This is why Shastri plays the role of puranik, why Dinakar takes the Ayyappa vow, why he feels so peaceful in Sitamma's presence, watching her lay the rangoli, watching her cook . . . For Dinakar, Sitamma's unquestioning acceptance of herself and her life are magical. As her son Narayan Tantri says, for her 'there will be no rebirth. She lives in this bhava without being of it.'

*

The solace available through experiences of timeless renewal, or through exposure to a peaceful, orderly life, is conveyed not only thematically but in the very language of *Bhava*. A lyrical intensity occurs in moments of transcendence, when the ego-bound, socially-defined self is immersed in something larger:

> 'What for thousands of years took form on the walls of temples and in the verandas of poor people's cottages, no matter how poor, had begun to manifest this morning on the veranda swept with cow-dung. A vine where one was necessary, and a leaf on the vine; for every leaf a flower, and a swastika to guard it all, and then peacocks, and then—look—there was Lord Ganesha, and even his mouse to ride on.'

> 'Nine triangles joining, one inside the other, creating an orbit which becomes a circle in turn becoming a chakra, the chakra becoming a petalled flower, the flower a form manifested within a square opened

out to the four directions, the whole figure wombing in itself the creative energy of earth and sky.'

'First, as if from the depths of a cave, one, one, or two, two, sprouts of melody, and now the clear sound of a bell emerging, and then a bass melody oooooo, and then jingling as if from belled anklets. All melody as if made from itself inside itself. As if going deeper and deeper down inside, melody wandering and searching the depth of the depths. Even as everything ended, again a melody arising from a deeper side of the kundalini. Did the melody find what it sought? As if saying look, look, the wonderment of small, small bells. Was it being lost, or drowning in ecstasy?'

'In the sky, the sun's love-play was over and the moon's grace appeared. While the sky seemed serene and peaceful, frothing waves moved over the sea, like thousands of white horses rushing forward in battle. The waves wet the feet of the two friends.'

With several significant exceptions, this blossoming into poetry is absent from descriptions of emotional and sexual relations between men and women. Although such relations (mostly Shastri's and Dinakar's) permeate the novel, they are more often a source of confusion and pain than of joy. (For the men, that is; we have little direct access to the intimate thoughts of any woman in the story, although Saroja's disgust is painfully apparent.) Consider Shastri's relations with his two wives, or the irony and brutal 'honesty' in Dinakar's letters to women with whom he has had an erotic connection. For each of these men, the involvement that most attracts beauty of language is the earliest and most innocent: Shastri with Radha, Dinakar with Gangu.

*

Language itself is also a theme in *Bhava*.

Anantha Murthy has commented that Indians live in an 'ambience of languages,' that the story plays with the notion of translation, and that the 'translation of events' was one of his preoccupations in this work. For example, translation comes into play when telling someone at home what happened in the workplace; or in telling something to one's mother, as opposed to a colleague. What is spoken in the home, in the street, in the office, on ritual occasions—all of these differ. And while the narrative of *Bhava* is in Kannada, to an exceptional degree the experiences of the characters originate in a multiplicity of languages: not only Kannada, but English, Hindi, Urdu. As well as sign language. And the languages of the heart. In many of the conversations, at least one character cannot use his or her mother tongue. Frequently, two or three characters converse only in a second language. Above all, at times there is no common language at all: so we have a Kannada narrative in which Dinakar, a major figure, cannot speak with a woman who is like his 'true mother' because she knows only Kannada, and he speaks none. Yet they communicate. In fact, that they do not share a language and still communicate so well emphasizes the deep connection between them.

Therefore the use, or mis-use, or circumventing of language becomes a metaphorical component of the novel, which is also about communicating: difficulties in communication echoed as difficulties in language.

*

Bhava is a departure for Anantha Murthy; he hasn't written any novel quite like it before. This may be a matter of disappointment to some readers who have come to expect from him work that is iconoclastic, rigorously challenging beliefs and practices, revealing forms that have lost their meaning—all of which characterize *Samskara*, for instance, and are absent from *Bhava*. The concern with crises of identity and spirit, although present and compelling in much of his earlier work, always has a dual purpose. The Acharya's spiritual crisis serves also as a microcosm of the crisis of identity in a whole community of brahmins. His rebirth takes place in a political/sociological context, necessitated by the surrounding religious and social decay. There is no such context in *Bhava*, which has a much smaller canvas; its crises of identity are not placed alongside the monoliths of community, society, tradition. The crises are simply there, products of individual defects in bhava; which is to say, products of being human. *Bhava* spotlights the individual caught in the web of being, of samsara. Everywhere there is evidence of samsara's illusoriness, the bane of 'not knowing': I don't know what is real. I don't know what 'real' means. I don't know who I am. I don't know whose father I am. I don't know whose son I am. I don't know what the 'I' in 'I am' means. So while the details of this novella are rooted in the Indian reality, the ultimate resonance is more immediately universal.

*

As in many traditional tales a question is raised; kept alive, despite possible solutions; maintained, till profounder questions are raised. Answers are delayed until the question is no longer relevant.

—A.K. Ramanujan on *Samskara*

Few of the mysteries in *Bhava* are ever resolved. The author's reluctance to solve them for us—his adopting a perspective that is diffused, not omniscient—is connected with the theme of 'not knowing,' and with the changing relevance of having questions answered. The characters move beyond the kind of resolution they required earlier, because critical changes take place in those most in need of a shift in their terms of being, most in need of a rebirth.

Shastri and Dinakar—who, especially if we think of the bhavavali, could be aspects of the same character enacting the same fate in different parts of the cycle—echo one another when abandoning their questions about paternity:

' "What does it matter if he is my son? Or if he is not?" Dinakar thought. "Whether I am his father, whether I am not, I should touch his feet." '

And Shastri thinks, of Dinakar,

' "Whether he is my son or not, he seems to be one who can give me a new life." '

By the end of *Bhava*, Shastri is, for the first time, benignly preoccupied with the future—his unborn grandchild and the reconciliation with his daughter. He begins to feel, wonderingly, tentatively, that even in old age he may yet, for a while, live without suffering and fury. The ordinary blessings might be his.

Prasad decides that he can live in the world

while not being of it. Having adopted the saintly simpleton, Chandrappa, as his spiritual father, he becomes unconcerned with the identity of his natural father, and loses his resentment of Narayan Tantri. In consequence, the pressure on Narayan Tantri to marry Gangu evaporates. Although Narayan Tantri is prepared to marry a woman born into the prostitute caste, Gangu herself comes to feel that the loving acceptance by Sitamma renders a public ritual unnecessary.

Dinakar, even without full awareness, has never before been so much among family: his 'other mother,' Sitamma; Shastri, who seems like 'a relation from some past life'; Prasad, in response to whom he experiences, for the first time in his life, the 'welling up of love for a child.'

When, at the end of his pilgrimage, Dinakar comes down from the hill and thinks, ' "That" is not to be won if you seek it wilfully,' he expresses an earned—if not completely experienced—response to Prasad's 'Who am I?'

'Thou art "That".' *Tattvamasi.*

Then he thinks of the evening when he 'became captive to Prasad's unshakable calm, and for a moment at least . . . was fully open, free of any desire or expectation.' He thinks of blessing Prasad—how it had seemed that Prasad ought to have been blessing him—and is in a state of exaltation.

The dazzle of illusion, even when we see through it; the ways in which we entangle ourselves, the ways in which we work free—

How do we get to change?

When all is said and done, it seems a matter of grace.

Notes

[The definition of 'bhava' given in the 'Translator's Note' is from *A Sanskrit-English Dictionary*, by Sir M. Monier-Williams.

In the Afterword, use is made of material from: *The Tibetan Book of Living and Dying*, by Sogyal Rinpoche, New Delhi: Rupa & Co., 1997; *The Tibetan Book of the Dead*, tr. Robert A.F. Thurman. London: Thorsons, 1995; *A Handbook of Tibetan Culture*, ed. Graham Coleman. New Delhi: Rupa & Co., 1995; and U.R. Anantha Murthy's *Samskara*, tr. A.K. Ramanujan. New Delhi: Oxford University Press, 1992.]

BOOK ONE

P.3 amulet: the amulet contains the Sri Chakra (also called Sri Yantra) diagram. A yantra is the manifestation of deity through visual form, and the Sri Chakra, a design of nine intersecting triangles, both embodies and makes manifest the goddess, the Divine Mother, 'Sri.' A way of referring to Lakshmi, Vishnu's consort, 'Sri' means prosperity, good fortune, auspiciousness. The type of Sri Chakra referred to here is inscribed on a scroll, consecrated, and kept inside an amulet; the amulet itself may bear a design as well.

P.4 Ayyappa pilgrim: Ayyappan (Shasta), the son of a union between Shiva and the enchantress Mohini (Vishnu in female form), is the presiding deity at the hill-top temple of Shabarimala in Kerala. Some devotees undertake a pilgrimage to the hill having sworn a vow that submerges their ordinary identity: they wear black clothing for the prescribed time, call one another only 'Swami,' observe dietary restrictions, forego alchohol, [sexual relations], and practice other austerities. Men of any age may visit the temple, but only women who do not menstruate (that is, young girls and women past menopause) are eligible [permitted]. Dinakar's choice of the Ayyappa pilgrimage (with its barring of women in their fertile years, and given Ayyappa's vexed parentage) may reflect areas of conflict in his own life.

tulsi: basil, which is sacred to Vishnu.

P.5 ritually pure things: 'madi,' the Kannada word for ritual purity, is also used in the text. (On page 20, Sitamma—having just bathed—is 'in a state of madi.')

P.6 harikatha: recitation and performance of stories from sacred literature, the lives of saints, and so on. Here, especially, 'stories of Hari' (one of Vishnu's names).

Kuchela: a poor boyhood friend of Krishna.

P.7 kuttavalakki and avalakki: both are based on pounded rice; kuttavalakki is fancier.

P.9 kirtanakar: singer of kirtans (devotional, religious songs).

P.10 Emden Boat: R.K. Narayan, in his book *My Days*, mentions the Emden Boat. 'Madras was bombarded by Emden in the First World War'; the commander of a German battleship 'had shelled Madras just for amusement.' Fearing that Madras would become another beachhead, some people in the coastal area fled inland. (New Delhi: Viking, 1996).

Shivalli Smrta, Shivalli Madhva: these represent a divergence in brahmin belief. Madhvas (followers of Madhvacharya) are dualists who worship Vishnu as the supreme god. Smrtas (followers of Shankaracharya, or Adishankara) are monists who do not, for example, consider Vishnu to be higher than Shiva. Shastri wears tulsi (sacred to Vishnu) in his topknot, and also wears rudraksha beads (sacred to Shiva). The compliment means that Shastri, though not subscribing to the hierarchy which regards Vishnu as supreme, is so expert at harikatha that he can evoke Krishna Paramatma (Vishnu) as if in a vision, even to Vishnu's own devotees. Shivalli is located in Udupi.

punya: merit, virtue (or reward for good acts).

P.14 'Shall I call you Chikappa, or Dodappa, or Mama?': these are all variations on 'uncle' ('Chikappa,' for example, is 'father's younger brother').

P.15 matra-raksha: protection (protective amulet) given by the mother.

P.17 'I have cultivated this addiction': i.e., reciting harikatha.

P.20 'What, Shastri-gale, why shouldn't I bathe again and then make your food?': Sitamma, having bathed, is in a state of 'madi,' ritual purity; if she touches Shastri, she will be polluted and must bathe again before cooking the meal which will be offered to god. 'Shastri-gale': ['gale' is an honorific].

P.22 'My Nani': 'Nani' is Sitamma's pet name for her son Narayan.

P.23 Venkatesha Stotra: hymn in praise of Lord Ventakesha (Vishnu) of Tirupati.

kadubu: a rice dish steamed in banana or jackfruit leaves.

P.24 the main oven opening sideways into another, and then another: the earthen stove has open flames of differing intensity. This variation is achieved by building a main ovenlike enclosure which has several holes through which fire is guided sideways, with diminishing intensity, into other chambers.

P.25 'If you had not taken this vrata, I would have waved drsti over you': ordinarily, Sitamma might wave something like chillies or incense around Dinakar's head to ward off the evil eye. But Dinakar does not need such protection; he is not in his ordinary state, because he has taken the Ayyappa vow (vrata: ritually—or self-imposed austerity; religious duty).

P.26 Vijayanagar Empire: comprised much of South India from the mid-fourteenth century for the next three hundred years. There is a belief that, when it fell, much of its treasure—especially in the form of gold—was looted.

P.27 'As soon as I saw the amulet, I knew that it contained a Sri Chakra': a Sri Chakra inscribed on a scroll is consecrated and kept inside an amulet; the amulet itself may bear a design as well. (See also note for page 3.)

P.27 Veda Vyas: by tradition the 'arranger[s]' or 'compiler[s]' of the Vedas (also of texts such as the Mahabharata and the Puranas).

P.30 'Prahlad or Dhruva': Both appear in Puranic tales as sons who, through devotion to Vishnu, overcome the rejection of their fathers.

P.30 Ekadashi: the 11th day of the moon, sacred to Vishnu, when orthodox brahmins observe a fast.

P.30 a goddess whom he had chosen for special devotion: his 'ishtadevata,' a chosen, or personal, deity with whom, from among the gods, one feels the closest (and perhaps least impersonal) connection; a tutelary deity believed to be especially concerned with one's welfare, something like a guardian spirit.

P.34 four upayas ('chaturupaya'; sama, dana, bheda, danda): 'Four strategies,' 'four tactics' for winning people over, Sama: friendliness, gentle persuasion. Dana: giving gifts or rewards. Bheda: divisiveness, fomenting differences among people. Danda: physical punishment.

P.40 Sharada: also Saraswati, goddess of music, learning.

P.48 'Such spirits make you roar "me me me" ': 'nanu, nanu, nanu' in Kannada (lit., 'P).

ishtadevata: see note for page 30.

P.48 kama, krodha, moha: lust, anger, attachment.

P.56 Trivikram: an epithet for Vishnu who, in his incarnation as a dwarf, asks the demon-king Bali for a small gift: the amount of land that can be measured off in three paces. When Bali agree, the dwarf makes himself enormous and—in just three strides—measures off the universe.

P.57 he had not yet completely become a wraith: since Radha persists in guarding Shastri's 'orthodoxy' in terms of eating taboos (which come into play because Shastri is a brahmin and Radha is a shudra), it means she doesn't see him as a wraith (pishachi), which has no caste at all.

P.58 received an omen from a lizard on the wall: refers to lore based on the interpretation of clicking sounds made by the lizard.

P.68 puranik: reciter of the Puranas.

BOOK TWO

P.74 'you speak to me in the Sahib's tongue?': Sitamma means Bombay Hindi, or Urdu; she associates Hindi-speakers with Muslims (because they are Northerners).

P.83 vairagya: indifference to worldly attachments; as if to say that Gangu has something of an ascetic streak in her.

kindari jogi: 'Pied Piper.' This tale, translated into Kannada, has been widely known for many years; it has been used, for example, in children's primers.

P.92 ichchamarani: 'one who can die when one wishes': for example, a sage possessing such power may inform his followers weeks beforehand of the date on which he will leave his body.

P.93 Adishankara: another name for Shankaracharya. See also note for page 10.

P.95 turning over: 'horalu,' in Kannada, suggests turning over, as when one is asleep.

P.96 the others lay down to sleep: on the pilgrimage, Dinakar has a separate sleeping-place, whereas the family (Sitamma, Narayan, Gopal and Gangu) would sleep in the same room.

P.97 samsara: worldly existence; the chain of births and deaths.

P.102 Appayya: Father. Prasad refers to Chandrappa alone as "father," even though he knows that Chandrappa is not his biological father.

P.109 Purana and pravacchan: 'purana' (lit. 'old'), a legend or story of ancient times, typically involving gods, heroes, sages, and so on. 'Pravacchan': sacred writings: discourse on religious teachings.

P.135 her cooking too was devoted to God: the Kannada text says that Sitamma was absorbed in her 'kayaka.' In this context, 'kayaka' means sanctified work, work offered to God; the concept is from Basava, a leader of the Virashaivite movement.

P.140 ' "Let Narayan Tantri begin coming home' . . . This was the first time he ever spoke my name to Gangu" ': Narayan is happy that his name is no longer taboo for Prasad, that at last Prasad will refer to him as something other than 'he' or 'that man.' Yet since, traditionally, no one speaks the name of his own father, it also emphasizes that Prasad does not regard Narayan as his father. (Prasad never calls Chandrappa—his self-chosen father—by name; he only calls him Appayya.)

BOOK THREE

P.148 Charvak: in a note to *Samskara* (p.152), A.K. Ramanujan mentions 'the Charvaka School, materialists and hedonist philosophers, who believed in the slogan . . . equivalent to "Enjoy yourself, even if it's on borrowed money." '

P.148 Charvak had gone even further than a Communist: Mangala is hinting that Charvak may be a terrorist, like a Naxalite.

READ MORE IN PENGUIN

In every corner of the world, on every subject under the sun, Penguin represents quality and variety—the very best in publishing today.

For complete information about books available from Penguin—including Puffins, Penguin Classics and Arkana—and how to order them, write to us at the appropriate address below. Please note that for copyright reasons the selection of books varies from country to country.

In India: Please write to *Penguin Books India Pvt. Ltd. 210 Chiranjiv Tower, Nehru Place, New Delhi, 110019*

In the United Kingdom: Please write to *Dept JC, Penguin Books Ltd. Bath Road, Harmondsworth, West Drayton, Middlesex, UB7 ODA. UK*

In the United States: Please write to *Penguin USA Inc., 375 Hudson Street, New York, NY 10014*

In Canada: Please write to *Penguin Books Canada Ltd. 10 Alcorn Avenue, Suite 300, Toronto, Ontario M4V 3B2*

In Australia: Please write to *Penguin Books Australia Ltd. 487, Maroondah Highway, Ring Wood, Victoria 3134*

In New Zealand: Please write to *Penguin Books (NZ) Ltd. Private Bag, Takapuna, Auckland 9*

In the Netherlands: Please write to *Penguin Books Netherlands B.V., Keizersgracht 231 NL-1016 DV Amsterdom*

In Germany : Please write to *Penguin Books Deutschland GmbH, Metzlerstrasse 26, 60595 Frankfurt am Main, Germany*

In Spain: Please write to *Penguin Books S.A., Bravo Murillo, 19-1'B, E-28015 Madrid, Spain*

In Italy: Please write to *Penguin Italia s.r.l., Via Felice Casati 20, I-20104 Milano*

In France: Please write to *Penguin France S.A., 17 rue Lejeune, F-31000 Toulouse*

In Japan: Please write to *Penguin Books Japan. Ishikiribashi Building, 2-5-4, Suido, Tokyo 112*

In Greece: Please write to *Penguin Hellas Ltd, dimocritou 3, GR-106 71 Athens*

In South Africa: Please write to *Longman Penguin Books Southern Africa (Pty) Ltd, Private Bag X08, Bertsham 2013*